Pri...
di...
Monrosa, announces his intent to abdicate the throne, they soon find themselves united in their royal duty.

And now they also have one more thing in common—their fight for true love! Because each of these princes is about to find themselves an unlikely princess. And they'll accept nothing less than governing their kingdom with their brides by their sides.

Discover Edwin's story in
Best Friend to Princess Bride

Read Luis's story in
Christmas Encounter with a Prince
Both available now!

And look out for Ivo's story
Coming soon!

Dear Reader,

Welcome to the second of the Royals of Monrosa trilogy. I had so much fun writing this book, whisking my characters from a Christmas in London to the Alpine ski slopes and then to the glamor and sophistication of a Mediterranean New Year's Eve ball.

Along the way, my characters Prince Luis of Monrosa and Alice O'Connor fall in love, a tender understanding for each other's troubled pasts bonding them. As I wrote this story, Luis's courage and integrity shone brightly and I couldn't help but fall totally in love with him. I hope you have a similar experience and cheer him on as he attempts to win Alice's heart.

Wishing you much care and kindness in your life.

Katrina

Christmas Encounter with a Prince

—

Katrina Cudmore

Recycling programs
for this product may
not exist in your area.

ISBN-13: 978-1-335-55648-6

Christmas Encounter with a Prince

Copyright © 2020 by Katrina Cudmore

This edition published by arrangement with Harlequin Books S.A.

For questions and comments about the quality of this book, please contact us at CustomerService@Harlequin.com.

Harlequin Enterprises ULC
22 Adelaide St. West, 40th Floor
Toronto, Ontario M5H 4E3, Canada
www.Harlequin.com

Printed in U.S.A.

A city-loving book addict, peony obsessive **Katrina Cudmore** lives in Cork, Ireland, with her husband, four active children and a very daft dog. A psychology graduate with an MSc in human resources, Katrina spent many years working in multinational companies and can't believe she is lucky enough now to have a job that involves daydreaming about love and handsome men! You can visit Katrina at katrinacudmore.com.

To Helen, for all the childhood memories.

CHAPTER ONE

ALICE O'CONNOR SHOT out of her chair as another thud sounded downstairs. Could it be burglars? Had some opportunist, on seeing the entire staff leave for their Christmas holidays earlier, decided now was the time to break into the London residence of the Monrosian Royal family?

She had to call the police. But where was her phone? Damn. She had deliberately left it downstairs to avoid wasting yet more valuable writing time internet browsing.

She glanced around the library for some form of weapon. But the only objects to hand were books. Thousands of them. She grabbed a sturdy hardback with sharp corners and crept towards the door.

She paused in the hallway, ears pinned back, but the faint sound of traffic out in Fitzalen Square was all that was to be heard.

She counted to ten, but no further noise came from downstairs. She lowered the book, doing a mental eye-roll.

The house was old and bound to creak and heave like an old ship. She swung around to return to the library. And froze. Her eyes widened. Downstairs a voice spoke. A male voice. Wait! That voice was familiar…deep and smooth with a sexy Mediterranean accent that sent a flow of heat through her body…a voice that had irritated and fascinated her with equal measure at her cousin Kara's wedding six months earlier.

She darted down the corridor and leant over the banister of the grand staircase.

It couldn't be. Oh, please, not him. Of all people, especially not him.

'Relax, Edwin, I promise to be in Monrosa for Christmas.' Silence followed and then he spoke even more impatiently. 'Yes, as soon as I take care of some business here in London.'

She leant further over the banister.

He was staying in London? Here?

'There's no need for security.' Silence followed that statement and then an exasperated breath. 'Don't blame them; I left the Bahamas without informing them. And I insist that you allow me some space—I don't need my protection team. I have to go, I have an urgent meeting.'

Beneath her, he appeared in the hallway, a hand raking through his dark, wavy hair, before he disappeared out of sight again.

She jerked back. The book leapt out of her hands. She went to grab it. Her fingertips glanced across the dark green woven cover but then it dropped fast and hard down through the stairwell. She stared after it and jumped when it smacked against the black and white tiles of the hallway two floors below.

She gasped and felt herself go the colour of a vine-ripened tomato.

A long silence followed and then slow footsteps. His feet came into view. It was the middle of winter. It was cold and wet. Then why on earth was he wearing flip-flops? He stepped forward, those broad shoulders lifting in question at the book sprawled on the floor. Pages had come loose.

Please don't make it a rare edition. My credit card will go up in flames if I try to load any more debt onto it.

His head lifted, and for a moment she was tempted to run back to the library and pretend that she had taken no part in events. But having backbone was everything to her. So, arranging her features into a blank expression, she waited for the humiliation to come.

As he studied her his puzzled expression only intensified and then shifted into incredulity. And then he laughed.

Indignation fired through her.

She dashed down the stairs towards him— Prince Luis of Monrosa, who was waiting at the bottom step for her with a grin and a raised eyebrow. She tried to slow down on the final turn of the stairs, suddenly feeling rather shy and ridiculous. But her momentum was too great and she hurtled towards him, expecting his glee at meeting once again the stranger who had ambushed and kissed him before fleeing into the night.

Alice O'Connor flew down the stairs towards him like a hacked-off doe, her long legs and arms performing an uncoordinated dance. Luis leapt forward, to save her from going head over tail, but at the last moment she sidestepped him.

'Your Highness, I didn't know… Kara told me that the house would be free for the entirety of the Christmas period. I have my PhD thesis to complete and need absolute solitude.'

So that explained why Kara's curious cousin was in the house.

Her black T-shirt had fallen off one shoulder, exposing a twisted black with red edging bra strap. He stared at it, a strange but strong compulsion to twist it back into place transfixing him. His hand moved out but just then she took the book that had dropped from the skies like a heat-seeking missile from him and added, 'You startled me.' She opened the book and leafed through the pages, her dark eyebrows knotting when she lifted the torn pages. 'Oh, no, I've damaged it.'

'What about me? I was almost impaled by it,' he pointed out.

That only earned him a brief shrug. Her hand stroked the cover of the book, her long fingers caressing the spine. He touched his neck to where her fingers had stroked his skin the night she had kissed him. 'You certainly know how to make an impression.'

Those grey eyes of hers lifted and she studied him with the same considered seriousness she had regarded him with at Edwin and Kara's wedding. He had only spoken to her, as they had waited for the newlyweds' departure for their honeymoon on the marina, because he had been concerned that she was about to fall into the sea, given how much she was swaying on her feet. At first he had thought she had drunk too much. But without him having said a word to this effect, other than to warn her of the water's edge, she had indignantly informed him that she had never touched alcohol in her entire life. Then, after serving him a rather impressive withering look, she had bent down, untied the strap of her sandal, stepped out of it, and yanked it out of where it had become stuck between the wooden planking of the jetty and had turned her back on him.

Her long brown hair had been tied up, faint freckles visible along her bare shoulders. He had shrugged and stepped away but then had turned back, intrigued by the fire in her eyes. She had reluctantly chatted with him after Edwin and Kara had left but had refused his invitation to dance with him back in the ballroom. He had forgotten about her and danced with other guests. But later that night when he had been walking through the gardens in search of his brother, Ivo, Alice had appeared before him. For a few seconds she had hesitated but then in the barest of whispers she had asked if she could kiss him. He wasn't given to kissing women he barely knew, it wasn't his style, but her quiet seriousness, her lack of pretence and flirtatiousness, had him nod yes, his amusement swiftly being replaced by intrigue and desire thanks to the mind-blowing, perfectly pitched kiss she had delivered. Tender, warm and full of promises.

But the moment his hand had brushed against her bare arm, the moment his mouth had opened to her parted lips, she had yanked back and walked away. When he had called out for her to stop she had given a firm shake of her head. By the time he had caught up with her, she was already in one of the cars taking guests to their nearby accommodation.

Now she lifted her chin, cleared her throat and offered, 'I believe I owe you an explanation.' She hesitated for a moment, her hands rubbing against the blue denim of her jeans. 'I've always wondered what it would be like to kiss a man with a beard. It was inappropriate of me and I hope I didn't offend you. It was a silly dare I had with one of my cousins. A silly dare and a silly mistake.'

A silly mistake.

Really?

He rubbed his hand against his jawline and said in a deliberately heavily accented and husky timbre, 'Am I safe now that my beard is gone…or do you want to see what it's like to kiss a guy with a day's worth of stubble?'

She blinked at that. Went to answer, but, her

eyes narrowing, realising he was teasing her, she asked instead, 'You're on your way to Monrosa? Are you leaving tomorrow?'

Her voice was full of hope.

He gave her a lazy grin. 'I haven't decided yet.' His gaze ran from her startled eyes, down over her high cheekbones and wide mouth, down over her lean body that only gave a hint of curves, down to her bare long and narrow feet, her toenails unpainted, a satisfying and pleasurable thought forming in his mind. 'I guess it depends on whether there's something better to keep me here in London.' Maybe Alice O'Connor was just the distraction he needed in his life right now.

'But surely you want to spend Christmas with your family. Kara told me that Edwin is looking forward to you all spending Christmas together this year. That it will be the first time in years.' Pausing, she frowned and asked, 'Why are you wearing shorts and flip-flops?'

Without answering her, he took the stairs down to the basement kitchen. Opening the fridge, he pulled out a beer. Alice appeared behind him. Popping the bottle open, he took a long, deep slug, his eyes never wavering from Alice's disapproving scowl. Dropping the bottle to the worktop, he looked at his watch. 'Twelve hours ago I was in the Bahamas. I decided I wanted a change of scene.'

'Couldn't you have at least changed your clothes?'

'I didn't have time.'

Her eyes widened and she edged away to stand on the other side of the kitchen island. 'Were you running away from something...or someone?'

He gave a chuckle. 'Just myself.'

'What do you mean?'

Well, Alice, I've just achieved my life's ambition—to win the Global Power Boat Championship Series. Right now I should be back in the Bahamas, celebrating with my team. But I tried that for a few hours and I couldn't stand it. I couldn't stand the thought of it all being over. I couldn't handle the prospect of saying goodbye to my team. Knowing that now I had to keep my promise to return to Monrosa and take up my royal duties.

Can you believe that I even considered messing up my last race and losing the championship so that I wouldn't have to honour that promise? That I was prepared to give up my life's ambition in order to avoid returning to Monrosa. To avoid a life of boredom and protocol and being under the constant scrutiny of

*my father. The man who couldn't even be both-
ered to call me and acknowledge my win. Like
a fool I had waited for hours for him to call.*

*But why had I expected him to do so, know-
ing just how much he disapproved of my career? Why had I expected him to be proud of
me, when I was nothing but a source of disappointment?*

He took another slug of beer. 'It was a joke.
You do get jokes, don't you?'

She eyed his now almost empty beer bottle
disapprovingly and answered, 'Yes, Your Highness, but only when the joke is explained to
me…really, really slowly.' Then, walking over
to the basement French windows, she pointed
out to the rain-soaked rear patio. 'Why on earth
would you want to come back here anyway?
It's wet and miserable. Surely a Mediterranean
palace or the Bahamas is preferable to this?'

She considered him, her hands reaching
around to rest in her back pockets. She was
cranky and unpredictable…but right now he
needed something that would distract him, and
Alice O'Connor would do nicely.

He finished his beer, set it down on the worktop and said, 'London does have its attractions.'
Moving towards her, he added in a low voice,
his eyes holding hers, 'Especially at Christmas

time, when everything is so beautiful. I like beautiful things. And you can call me Luis... I think we've already moved beyond the formal, don't you?'

Alice could understand why so many women fell for Luis. When it came to a checklist of desirable must-haves, he had them all. A prince. *Tick*. Tall, dark and handsome. *Tick*. A charismatic sports star who was at the top of his game and lauded for his commitment and bravery. *Tick*. A man with the unerring but addictive ability to make you feel as if you were the most important person in the world by holding your gaze with those soft hazel eyes and smiling gently at you. *Tick*.

But beneath the veneer of all those deceptively attractive qualities she was certain that he was just like her dad—self-regarding, self-centred and driven at all costs. And with those traits came manipulation and pain for those surrounding them. Which made the fact that she had kissed him all the more confusing and galling. At times since Kara's wedding she had been able to convince herself that the kiss was all about her gaining control of that strange chemistry he had stirred up in her, but at other times she had had to admit to herself that it had been nothing more than ill-advised lust. And she hated herself for it. She hated losing control. She hated deviating even an inch from the life she had planned out for herself. And Luis had sent her careering off that path, okay only for a few crazy minutes, but it had seriously unsettled her. And it wasn't going to happen again.

She held out her hand. 'How about we start again… Luis?'

He took her hand and, giving her one of those heart-melting smiles of his, he said, 'It is the season of goodwill after all.'

His grip was strong, his skin warm. A buzz ran up her arm and down her entire body. Flustered, she snatched her hand away. 'Can I take it that you are yet another fan of Christmas? Don't you get bored of it? It's the same dingdong every year, the same songs that are so sappy they make my skin crawl. Not to mention the same crazy buying of gifts that nobody wants. A law should be introduced whereby only under-tens are allowed to celebrate Christmas. Everyone else should have to just grow up and go to work. Think about just how unproductive it all is.'

He gave a chuckle and shifted closer to her. 'My, aren't you a modern-day Miss Scrooge?' Something dark and mischievous glinted in his eyes. 'Maybe you need to be shown just how magical Christmas can be.'

His voice was low, sexy. Beneath his black sailing fleece his pink polo shirt was open at the neck, revealing a fine dusting of dark hair and tanned skin. Something warm stirred in her veins.

'I'm going to a party after I shower and change; why don't you come with me…' he paused, his lips curled up into an even more seductive smile '…to the party, I mean?'

What would it be like to watch him undress? Watch him step into the shower? Follow him into the warmth of the water? Get to know his body?

She jerked away from him. What on earth was the matter with her? She had a schedule to keep. A word-count to maintain. She had ten days to get her PhD thesis under control. Ten days of hiding away from the world, ten days of thankfully being able to avoid the silly season that was otherwise known as Christmas. Ten days before she would have to return to work and the erratic temperament of her boss at the coffee shop. And two weeks until her next meeting with her university supervisor, who, given the tone of their last catch-up, was seriously starting to question Alice's ability to complete her thesis. And no PhD would mean she could kiss goodbye to any hope of securing a full-time lecturing position. She shouldn't be wasting time having schoolgirl fantasies about her cousin's brother-in-law. A real-life Prince Charming who was born to break women's hearts. 'Sorry, but I'm busy. I have to focus on my thesis.'

His head tilted. 'That's a shame…it's Christmas, after all. You should be enjoying yourself.' The teasing disappearing from his eyes, he added, 'I'll feel bad leaving you here all on your own. Are you sure you won't come?'

For a moment she actually thought he was being sincere. The tone of his voice, the gentleness in his expression almost fooled her. She had to give it to him, he was a seriously good actor. But she trusted Prince Luis just about as far as she could throw him—and, given that he must be close to six feet four, and therefore had a seven-inch advantage over her, she wouldn't be able to throw him far. He was trying to charm her. Why was beyond her, as they had nothing in common and it wasn't as if there was a shortage of woman keen to date him if media reports were anything to go by. But she didn't have the time or interest in working that particular puzzle out. Not with a PhD to complete.

And the idea of attending a Christmas party frankly left her feeling cold. All that forced and pretend gaiety. When in truth for many Christmas was about bickering and arguing, the unleashing of simmering tension and anger. She grabbed Luis's empty beer bottle and rinsed it at the sink, before wiping it dry. Dropping it into the recycling, she answered, 'I have a schedule I have to keep.'

Opening the fridge door, he considered its contents. 'It's Christmas. Everyone should forget about schedules and work at Christmas.'

'Not me. I don't do Christmas.'

He shut the door with a frown. 'So I gathered.' Spotting the tin of chocolates on the counter beside the fridge, he prised the lid open. Alice winced. He rifled through it, his frown deepening. 'Who eats all of the chocolates and leaves the wrappers behind?'

Earlier, after she had deleted all her day's pathetic word-count, she had tossed herself into the tin of Christmas chocolates her mother had sneakily hidden in her luggage. There was no way a professional sportsman would understand how a grown adult could devour an entire tin of chocolates in one afternoon thanks to bored frustration, so she wasn't even going to bother trying. So instead she backed towards the kitchen door and said, 'If I don't see you tomorrow before you leave for Monrosa…well, it's been nice seeing you again. Enjoy your time with your family. Give my love to Kara.'

Unwrapping a chocolate in a purple foil wrapper that he must have found at the bottom of the tin, he gave a resigned shrug and said, 'If you change your mind then you can join me at the Stewart Club. I'll leave your name at the door.'

About to head up the stairs, she paused. His party was at the Stewart Club? Where it was said that Lady Radford had frequented. She'd love to have the opportunity to see the interior of one of London's oldest and most exclusive private clubs. She eyed Luis. But to do so would mean accepting his invite. She moved back into the kitchen. Watched as he popped the dark chocolate into his mouth, his eyes lighting up with delight as he savoured the praline inside.

She should turn around. Go back up to the library. But instead she heard herself say, 'My thesis is on the writer Lady Maud Radford. She used to dine frequently in the Stewart Club— in fact, it's said that it was there she found the opportunity to influence those in government at the time with her political and social-reform ideas. So in the name of research I would like to join you tonight. But only for a short while. And strictly on a work basis.'

He laughed at that. 'Do you ever chill out, Alice?'

She gave him a death stare. 'I'll change and be working in the library when you've finished your beauty regime.' Climbing the stairs to his laughter, she groaned. Hating just how prickly she became at Christmas. Hating how prickly she was when life took an unexpected turn.

CHAPTER TWO

'So, YOUR THESIS, tell me…' Luis had no sooner returned to his seat beside her when he was interrupted once more. Standing up, he gave her an apologetic smile before kissing both women in the group on the cheek and back-slapping the three men, laughter and chatter dancing between them.

Sitting back into her chair, Alice decided a Christmas party at the Stewart Club would make for a great social anthropology study. Somehow, without any formal organisation, those attending understood where they stood in the social hierarchy. Those on the lower social rungs were the ones who were expected to travel the thronged room, greeting those higher up the ladder, who stayed put in the vicinity of their table. And, of course, Prince Luis of Monrosa was the prize person to talk to tonight. Within minutes of their arrival at the club, Luis had been drawn into an unending cycle of greeting acquaintances and friends. Not once had he failed to recall a name, and his keen attention on everyone he spoke to only seemed to up the excitement and general air of goodwill and celebration in the room.

How easily people fell for the affirmation of attention. What was it in us humans that needed the acknowledgement of others? Even when it was to our detriment? After her parents' divorce, even when she had known for years the ugly side to her father, she had craved his attention. Believed that this time things might be different. How many times had he not turned up to meet her? Or turned up steaming drunk? How many times had she forgiven him when he told her he was sorry and that he would never let her down again? He had been so charming and funny and warm. A born entertainer. In his good moments he'd made life seem magical. But then he would drink and become bitter and belligerent and blame her for not understanding him.

Now she smiled as a waiter placed a pot of tea and teacup on the table. With Luis otherwise occupied she had earlier explored the club, taking in the historic rooms upstairs, the gallery and library, taken photos of the grand dining room with its heavy chandeliers and dark wood panelling, imagining Lady Radford dining there.

When she had finished her tour of the club she had dithered in the hallway before eventually deciding to join the party, the guilt of not meeting her writing milestones losing out to the temptation of spending more time in the place where Lady Radford had socialised in the vain hope it might just provide her with the inspiration she desperately needed to get over her writing slump.

Around her champagne and laughter flowed. Out on the dancefloor guests danced to the DJ's Christmas playlist. When she had returned to the main party, which was taking place in the reading room of the club, Luis had gestured for her to join him and he had introduced her to the people he was talking to with great enthusiasm. Several times he had sat beside her and begun a conversation but time and time again he had been interrupted. Watching him now, gesturing wildly, those around him wide-eyed at whatever story he was telling them, she marvelled at the fact that earlier, on their way to the party, he had admitted to being jet lagged. But nobody would guess that now. For a moment she wondered what it must be like to be so carefree, so open to others, but then she remembered that the outer persona so often masked the truth of the inner person.

Dressed in black tie like all of the other male guests, Luis had assured her that her choice of a knee-length black dress was perfect for the party...which was a good thing, as that and a leather skirt were the only half-decent items she had brought with her to London. Unfortunately, however, all the other female guests were dressed in festive golds and silvers and reds and she had been stopped several times in her tour of the club and given a drinks order. She didn't belong here amongst all the glitz and glamour and bonhomie.

His story over, Luis turned to a woman standing to his right. Bowing his head, he whispered something into her ear. The woman nodded and then, curving into him, flung her arms around his neck. They embraced well beyond what was socially polite.

She placed her teacup down on the saucer. It was time she left.

Standing, she grabbed her bag.

'I'm not being a good host, am I?'

She shrugged, looking away from Luis's apologetic smile. Hating how easily he could make her heart leap with just a smile. 'I didn't expect you to play host. I only came to see the inside of the club. And now it's time for me to go home.'

His hand touched against her arm. 'Stay and dance with me. I do want to hear about your thesis.'

With a grin he removed his tuxedo jacket and threw it on his chair. She wanted to say no. This was not how she had planned out her trip to London. And something way too giddy was stirring in her blood at the gorgeous shape of his torso beneath his shirt—incredibly broad shoulders tapering down to a narrow waist. For a person with embarrassingly limited experience when it came to men, the effect Prince Luis of Monrosa was having on her was baffling beyond all measure. She *should* leave. *But* she was staying in his family's home. Wouldn't it be impolite for her to refuse to dance with him?

She nodded and he held out his hand to her. Inhaling deeply, she took it and allowed him to lead her out onto the dance floor, trying to resist the urge to grab her hand back out of his grasp, the heat, the strength, the callused skin of his hand disturbing reminders of the raw maleness that lay just below his outward display of the equable Royal Prince.

On the dance floor she groaned when Luis began to dance. Damn it, but he could move. Whereas she, as her friend Toni liked to joke, danced like a giraffe on acid. Luis's hips swayed, his arms moved in time with the beat, his eyes fixed on hers, inviting her to join him. She gave her hips a tiny sway. He nodded encouragingly. She moved her hips in a wider circle, trying to smile and pretend it all came naturally. She lifted her arms and shuffled her feet, bumping into Luis in the process. He placed a steadying hand on her waist, his eyes dancing with amusement. Was he aware that her breast was squashed against his arm?

'I'm starting to think that this is going to be a particularly good Christmas.'

She arched her neck away from the warmth of his breath, her pulse whooshing in her ears at the huskiness of his voice. His hands shifted ever so slightly, his thumbs fixing on the points of her hips. His scent was like a mixture of freshly washed cotton and earthiness…with a pinch of goodness.

She stared at the crisp whiteness of his dress shirt, thrown by just how wrong it was that someone so dangerous could smell so…pure and right. He weakened her. Something about him stirred a chemistry inside her that she seemed incapable of controlling. Now, for the first time in her life, she understood why people took reckless decisions that went against everything they strove for.

She shifted her gaze upwards, knowing it was time to stay goodnight, when a commotion to the side of the room had her shift her attention in that direction instead.

A group of middle-aged men were making their way into the room, calling out to a friend who was standing at the bar. She gasped. Pulled herself away from Luis. At the centre of the group, his arms thrown around his companions on either side, was her father. She knew by the gleam in his eye, the high colour in his cheeks, that he was drunk.

This could not be happening. She needed to run…but her feet felt as though they were glued to the floor. The DJ played a new track, killing the men's overbearing voices. She was vaguely aware of Luis asking her if she was okay.

And then her father looked in her direction.

She twisted away, crouching over. A service entrance was in front of her. She stumbled towards it, panic pounding in her ears.

Dio! Didn't she realise he was only flirting with her? Luis watched Alice run from the room, pushing past startled partygoers, heard their surprised laughter at her desperation to leave. For a moment he considered just letting her go. Alice O'Connor unsettled him. She was impossible to read. Up to a minute ago she had seemed to be enjoying the night…in her own quiet way. But now she was bolting away—just as she had done at the wedding. But he couldn't let her go without at least seeing her to the safety of a taxi.

Chasing after her, he raced through an empty service corridor and then the club's kitchen, and outside the kitchen's double swing doors he saw Alice in the distance at the main entrance door.

He called out her name, but she disappeared outside.

It was raining hard. Raindrops bounced off the footpath. He cursed as a passing black cab sprayed him. Shoes soaked, he stared after Alice, who was sprinting down the street. Couldn't she at least have collected her coat before rushing away?

'Alice!'

Passing traffic and the heavy rain meant she probably couldn't hear him. He broke into a run, a car horn blaring when he crossed a side street without looking. Ahead Alice was slow-ing as she waved frantically for a cab to stop, but they all rushed by, already occupied.

He was fast gaining on her when she turned a corner into a pedestrian side street. He followed her, the rain pinning his dress shirt to his skin. He cursed and stopped. The street was empty. Where had she disappeared to?

'Alice!' His call echoed down the narrow shopping street, the blue and white overhead Christmas lights swaying in the breeze.

He shouted her name again. 'Alice!' This time more angrily, panic taking hold. What if something happened to her? How well did she know London? He broke into a jog. There were several arcades and narrow lanes leading off the street. She could have gone down any of them.

He bellowed her name again, frustration adding to his panic.

And then he saw her. Pushed into the furthest reaches of a darkened doorway, shivering, her eyes that of a hunted animal.

He came to a stop. Waited for her to come out. But instead she cowered even more into the darkest recesses of the store. She was terrified. Of him? Had he triggered something in her?

'Please don't shout.'

He flinched at the desperation in her voice.

He took a step backwards, holding his hands up.

I won't do you any harm.

'I was worried—that's why I was shouting.'

For long seconds she considered him. He waited for her to speak, to explain what was going on. But it seemed as though she was incapable of speech.

'You need to be indoors.' He held out a hand, wanting to lead her out of that dark and cold place she was hiding in, but she didn't react. He took the smallest of steps forward, lowered his voice. 'I'll take you wherever you want to go—a friend's house or a hotel if you don't want to return home with me.' He let out a long exhale. 'I'm sorry, Alice; I've upset you. Let me make this right.'

She shook her head. 'It wasn't you.'

Then what? He wanted to ask a hundred questions but knew he had to wait until she was ready to talk.

She stepped out of the doorway, wrapping her arms tight against her waist. 'Can you find me a cab?' Her hair was soaked through, its heavy weight emphasising the height of her cheekbones, the almond shape of her eyes. Her long, narrow frame seemed so fragile he longed to pull her into a hug, to make things right for her. Which, of course, was the last thing he should do right now. She nodded in the direction of the club, and added, 'You must return to the party…' Her eyes flicking over him and lingering for a moment on his rain-saturated shirt, she grimaced. 'I'm so sorry, I didn't mean for you to follow me out. I've ruined the night for you.'

He shook his head and gestured that they should walk back in the direction they had come from. He waited until they were out in the main street, where there were people walking by, wanting her to have the security of having other people nearby before he said, 'I don't understand what has just happened, but I do want to help.'

Her eyes flickered towards him, studied him for a few seconds and then moved away. A shudder ran through her body. 'I saw someone… I thought he was chasing me.' Those grey eyes of hers that were so wary and cautious met his again, an apologetic smile trembling on her lips. 'I didn't realise it was you… and now you're soaked through.'

He wanted to know who she had seen. Who had terrified her so much? He wanted to go back to the club and thump whoever had caused this fear in her. But instead he waited until a black cab appeared down the street and, stepping out into the road, he forced it to stop. The driver wound down his window and started to hurl a barrage of abuse in his direction. Luis interrupted him by pulling out his wallet and withdrawing a large number of notes. Calmly he explained that it was an emergency, and on the offer of a substantial sum of money both the driver and two male occupants happily agreed to Alice and him taking the cab, the two men heading in the direction of a nearby pub.

He instructed the cab driver to drive around the block while he phoned ahead to the club. As they pulled up to the door, Jana, the general manager at the Stewart, ran down the steps with both of their overcoats.

He helped Alice into her black wool coat and, despite her resistance, insisted that she use his as a blanket.

They travelled back to Mayfair, passing by the Natural History Museum and Hyde Park, both decked in festive lights, in silence. He clenched his fists to stop himself from reaching for Alice, who despite the coats was still shivering fiercely. He wanted to make all of this better for her.

Outside a department store, people were

standing on the pavements looking at the Christmas scenes in the window fronts. He had hoped for a night where he could forget about the life, the friends and team he was leaving behind and the unwanted future that stood in front of him. But instead he had half frightened his house guest to death. Yet another example of him getting things wrong.

'I'm ashamed to be your father.'

His father's words to him as a fourteen-year-old boy. Words only uttered once, but conveyed ever since in every look and criticism of his life choices. In his father's eyes he brought shame on the family and Luis did nothing to combat his father's opinion, wanting to antagonise him, wanting to hurt him as much as his father's behaviour in the aftermath of his mother's death had scarred him. They had once been close, had shared a passion for sport. Intuitively they had understood one another, mirroring each other's personality. They were both outspoken, impetuous, extrovert. But after his mother's death his father had withdrawn into himself, had become ever more defensive and irritable. Their once close relationship had crumbled and Luis had learnt the fickleness of love. He had learnt to never fully engage with or trust another person. He had learnt that you never truly know what others were truly thinking and wanting and feeling, beyond the smoke and mirrors that collapsed in a moment of crisis. He had learnt that a life lightly led, a transitory life, was far more preferable to one where you overly relied on others. He was never going to overly rely on another person again and he certainly wasn't going to allow a relationship to destroy him as had happened to his father following his mother's death.

Sure, he had a reputation for dating countless women, but that reputation was media-driven and one he didn't go out of his way to dispel, given how much it maddened his father. He enjoyed socialising. Had a large circle of friends. He adored the buzz, the distraction of other people; it suited his personality…and the need to forget the hole inside himself.

A hole that Alice O'Connor's reserved and watchful presence made a whole lot bigger as though she were holding a magnifying glass up to it.

He offered her a smile. And his heart tugged when she attempted a smile in return, heat flaming in her cheeks. She looked away towards the lights of Green Park and the groups of people heading to the nightlife in Piccadilly, but not before he saw tears glisten in her eyes.

The cab swung down a side street, the passing street lights flickering over the soft, full shape of her lips, the long, straight line of her nose, the sweep of her eyelashes, the darkness of her brows, that perfectly framed her once again closed and reserved expression.

He reached out his hand, resting it next to where her hand lay on his coat. She startled when his finger touched hers, an inch of skin on skin.

Her gaze swept back to meet his; it was wary, as though she was trying to gauge whether she could trust him. He tried to shrug off the disappointment that came when her hand shifted away.

Alice walked to her bedroom door. Stopped. Spun around. Paced the soft, dove-grey carpet, circling the blush-pink two-seater sofa at the centre of the room. She owed Luis a proper apology and explanation. But should she wait until the morning, when she'd be less emotional?

The past hour had been nothing short of a nightmare. Luis must think that she was completely unstable. The first time they met she had ensnared him in a kiss and tonight she had bolted out of the party with no explanation.

How was she going to explain her behaviour to him, without having to unearth memories and feelings she wanted to keep buried? It wouldn't be so hard if he had just been disbelieving and impatient with her like her ex, Rory, had used to be when her dad would call her phone number. It was over a decade ago but Rory's irritation with her fears, how he'd used to ask her if she was sure that her dad was as bad as she claimed he was, had made her question her own sanity and her memories and reading of her own life. No wonder their relationship hadn't lasted more than a year. And since then her romance history had consisted of a litany of disastrous first dates, that she had half-heartedly gone on in the first place, giving into her best friend Toni's insistence that she couldn't remain single for ever. Her dates had included guys she had thought were lovely and kind at first, who made her feel hopeful but then would let slip towards the end of the night that they were already in a relationship. Others had thought it was okay to lie about most things—their age, their job and their interests—in order to secure a date. The guy who had given Toni the best laugh was the one who had turned up to the restaurant carrying a bag of 'leather items' he thought they might use later that night. Alice had walked straight out, swearing never to look at a dating app again.

She approached the bedroom door again, placed her hand on the doorknob and took a deep breath. She was his guest. The least she could do was apologise again for dragging him away from the party early. She closed her eyes, remembering the image of him standing on the pavement, the irritation in his eyes, in the tight scowl on his mouth, softening to concern. The street light had flashed on the beads of water dripping down the sharp edges of his face, his soaked shirt stuck to his torso like a second skin. For a moment she had wanted to weep with relief that he was there for her. But thankfully she had pulled herself up on that particularly delusional hope—her judgement on men had been disastrous in the past and she could see zero reason why that would have changed now. Especially with a thrill-seeking, restless prince with a reputation for playing the field.

She found him in the basement kitchen. He had showered too and was now dressed in grey cotton lounge pants and a navy long-sleeved top. Leaning against the kitchen counter, he was eating trifle from a crystal serving bowl, not pausing when she appeared.

'Would you like some?' he asked, nodding to the bowl.

'I don't like custard.'

'All year or just in protest at Christmas?'

Despite her nerves, or perhaps because of them, she laughed. He raised an eyebrow. No wonder. Her laugh was bordering on hysterical.

Using her sopping dress as an excuse to escape, she took refuge in the adjacent laundry room and tried to gather herself as she placed it in the washing machine.

Back in the kitchen once again, she found Luis now tucking into a fist-sized piece of Christmas pudding covered in a small mountain of cream.

Shaking her head when he offered her some, she cleared her throat. 'I'm sorry about earlier… I really thought it was someone else following me.' A drop of water from her hair oozed down onto her pyjama top. She shivered in memory of how cold she had felt as she had hidden in the shop doorway.

He nodded to the counter behind her. 'I made you a pot of tea. There's milk in the fridge if you take it—I'm assuming you don't take sugar.'

Tea was exactly what she wanted. But why was he making the assumption that she didn't want sugar? 'Why would you think that?'

Amusement shone in his eyes. 'Because I reckon you like to do everything by the book, including having a clean diet...' his eyes trailed over to the chocolate tin on the counter '...although perhaps at times, despite yourself, you are human like us all and give in to temptation.'

She tried to pretend she had no idea what he was talking about and poured some tea. God, was she that obvious? Well, they said sugar was good for shock. Opening the kitchen cupboard where she knew the sugar was kept, she took down the silver canister and put a teaspoon into her cup.

Approaching the fridge, which Luis was standing in front of as though guarding its contents, she said, 'I need the milk.'

Opening the fridge, he took out a milk carton and was about to pour it into her cup when he stopped and said gently, 'Why don't you put it down on the counter?'

Damn. She hadn't realised that her hands were trembling so badly. It was as if the cold from earlier had seeped into her bones. And as he poured the milk into her cup she realised just how tired she was. Not just because of what'd happened tonight, but she was tired to her bones trying to work full-time in the café, sometimes working double shifts to pay her rent and trying to complete her PhD. And she realised just how nice it was to have someone to do something as simple as make her a cup of tea. Living alone gave her the independence she craved…but a solo life had little softness. There was no one to cheer you up on a bad day, to help pick up the pieces when things went wrong.

With a smile that undid her with its soft kindness, Luis pushed the teacup in her direction.

Shifting back to the other side of the kitchen island, she sipped the tea, trying to keep her expression neutral when the overly sweet liquid made her want to grimace.

She took another sip, preferring the sickly taste to explaining why she had fled from him earlier. But Luis deserved some honesty. 'I…' She paused, a heat spreading from her stomach out onto her skin. 'I saw my father tonight, at the club. We don't speak.'

'You're scared of him?'

She inhaled at his question. 'Scared, no…' She wanted to turn away, say goodnight. Forget about her father.

'Do you want me to call the police?'

'No. No, nothing like that. I just got a shock.

I didn't expect to see him. My aunt had told me that he had moved to France a few years ago to be a rugby coach at a club there. I didn't want to speak to him—it never turns out well when we do. I needed to get away, and when you followed me out of the club I thought you were him.'

'I'm sorry that I scared you.'

She smiled at that. 'You're not the one who should be apologising. I ruined your night.'

'There'll be plenty more of them—don't worry.'

Was there a hint of boredom in his voice? But she shook off that thought. Why would there be? Luis was a party animal.

'Has he hurt you, Alice?'

The gentleness of his voice grabbed her by the heart. Crazy tears filled her eyes. The stress of her PhD was getting to her. She swallowed hard. 'No…not really.' And then she made the mistake of looking up to see Luis move across the kitchen to stand opposite her. Not too close, but near enough for her to see the lines of tension at the sides of his mouth.

'He's an alcoholic, not that he'd admit to that. He used to be a professional rugby player. He had to retire early due to injury and found a friend in alcohol. He never hurt me…'

She stopped, her heart pounding. Remembering the arguments, the thuds and the silence downstairs that would follow. How her mother would try to cover up her bruises the following day.

'But he did hurt others…your mum?'

She nodded at that. Her heart pulling apart to remember how her mum had used to try to pretend it never happened. Her shame of it transferring to Alice. It was something not to be spoken about. How could the town's famous son, Freddie O'Connor, possibly be a domestic abuser? He was the genius rugby player who charmed everyone in his wake. Even his wife and daughter found it hard to comprehend the dichotomy in his personality.

'We don't have to talk about it if you don't want to, Alice.'

She nodded, grateful that he wasn't going to push her, and touched her hair, glad to have an excuse to get away. 'I need to dry my hair.' She went to move away but stopped. 'Thank you for being so…so kind tonight.'

He made an amused sound. 'You sound surprised.'

'I guess.'

'Maybe we have misjudged one another.'

Taken aback, she studied him for a moment,

the seriousness in his expression making her wonder who the true Prince Luis of Monrosa was. Had she totally misread him? Perhaps.

'Sleep well…and be kind to yourself; none of this was of your making.'

She nodded to his quietly spoken words, and climbed the stairs, her heart pounding in her chest at how utterly dangerous and beguiling he was.

CHAPTER THREE

ONE HUNDRED PER cent focus. That was what she needed to give this thesis. Plain and simple. Just get the words down and forget about that voice in her head that was telling her to give up, that she was an imposter and that there was no way she was going to finish it.

For God's sake, Alice, are you going to crumble now, when finishing it is within your grasp? Where has your fire, your determination disappeared to? Where's your passion for this career that has consumed you for the past decade? Remember how you used to say you'd prove the father who had told you that you were wasting your time on a subject with zero employment possibilities wrong when you made something of yourself?

She scrolled through the pages and pages of her already written words on her laptop screen, barely remembering writing them—it was as though they belonged to someone else.

She breathed against the panic in her chest. She was scared. Scared of not finishing this. Scared of what her future would look like. What if she didn't get a lecturing position? How many years would she have wasted chasing that dream? And what if she did get a position and it wasn't what she wanted after all?

Her passion for history was gone.

As evidenced by today. Here she was, sitting in a near empty reading room in the British Library, with its perfect lighting, silence and soothing architecture for inspiration. But instead of producing a blockbusting word count she was just faffing about. She knew what sections of the thesis she needed to address. There were gaps in her exploration and analysis of Lady Radford's writing and advocacy on the right to a free education for all. In her head she knew the points she wanted to make, but articulating them, actually typing the words, was proving impossible.

She closed her eyes. Breathed deeply.

Don't panic. You have this under control. You are strong.

She shrank inside herself, a series of images floating in the darkness behind her lids. Christmas Eve in her childhood home. The year her dad had been away all summer. The laughter.

The unspoken disbelief that this year things might be different. They had gone Christmas shopping together and afterwards had eaten in their local Chinese restaurant. But on their way out he had bumped into some fans, complete strangers to him, who had persuaded him to join them for a drink in a local bar. Her mother had pleaded with him. Had cried when she had driven herself and Alice home. Alice had woken in the early hours of Christmas morning to the sound of her mother's scream for him to get out and then the sound of her body slamming against a wall.

She ground her teeth, anger flaring inside her. He had ruined her childhood. He was *not* going to ruin her future.

She needed to delve deeper into Lady Radford's influence on government policy.

But instead an uncomfortable thought and accompanying heat flamed her skin. Luis had come to her rescue last night—a fact she was grateful for, but she hated that he had seen her so weak. It was a side of herself she kept hidden from everyone. Even herself. Why was she so vulnerable these days? Was it tiredness? The uncertainty over her future?

'Finally! There you are. I've been searching for you.'

Alice leapt in her chair and screamed. Opening her eyes, she blinked hard.

What on earth was Luis doing here and why did he look so pleased with himself?

From somewhere across the room, someone made a disapproving tutting sound.

Pulling out the chair next to her, Luis sat, his grin growing wider. He tutted too. And, those hazel eyes of his sparkling with amusement, he leant into her and whispered, 'Are you a screamer, Alice?'

She tried not to redden.

Act blasé. If he knew the truth, would he laugh?

'What are you doing here?'

He rocked back in his chair. 'Now, that sounds like you're unhappy to see me. Do you know just how difficult it was to persuade Security to allow me in here?' He raised both arms into the air, stretching long and luxuriously, gave a yawn. 'I found your note saying you were going to work here for the day, so I decided I'd come and take you to lunch.'

'Aren't you supposed to be travelling back to Monrosa right now?' She didn't mean to sound so peeved, but the sight of Luis stretching like a giant and powerful cat, sending unfair pheromones into the air, made her feel irritable.

Eyes on her blank computer screen, he shrugged. 'There's no rush.'

She angled the laptop out of his line of sight. 'I'm busy.'

He smiled at that, raised a disbelieving eyebrow. 'It sure seemed like a flurry of activity when I arrived.'

'What do you want, Luis?'

Placing an elbow on the desk and resting his head in his hand, he studied her for a few moments, his expression now earnest. 'To make sure you're okay before I leave.'

'I told you this morning that I'm fine.' Earlier, as she had been heading up to the library, Luis had come out of his bedroom, all sleepy eyes and tousled hair, and in a husky voice had asked why on earth she was up so early.

For a fraction of a moment she had wondered what it would be like to follow him back into the darkness of his bedroom, feel his arms wrap around her, have his mouth on hers once again.

And their eyes had met and something raw and elemental had spun between them.

Heart thumping, she had turned away from him, terrified of just how vulnerable she felt around him. And when she had heard him leave the house later in the morning, irritated by just how skittish and distracted she had been all morning at the thought of him sleeping down-stairs, she had flung her laptop and notes into her bag and fled for the sanctuary of the Brit-ish Library.

'I know a great Peruvian restaurant close by—I'm sure the break will do you good.'

She didn't deserve a lunch break. Not with such a dismal word output today. She was about to say no, but the concern in Luis's gaze had her reluctantly stand and nod her acceptance. Her behaviour last night had obviously alarmed him greatly; she needed to prove to him that he could leave London with a clear conscience and that she would be okay on her own. With Luis gone, then just maybe the words would come.

Beyond the Christmas lights surrounding the restaurant window, head bowed, her phone to her ear, Alice paced the Marylebone foot-path. They had just ordered their food when her phone had rung, and with a concerned ex-pression she had excused herself and stepped outside.

Okay, so he knew by taking Alice to lunch that he was procrastinating. Putting off travel-ling back to Monrosa. But being in Monrosa agitated him. How the hell would he cope with living there full-time? Palace life stifled him.

It made him feel like a shadow of his true self. Royal expectation and formality choked him. It was as though he had to suppress every truth about himself. But he had promised his father... and, despite what his father thought, he did not go back on promises. Maybe it was because of his father's low opinion of him, but integrity and honour were vital to his self-regard and esteem.

Outside, Alice placed her phone in the back pocket of her jeans. But didn't come back inside. Instead she seemed to stare blankly at all of the last-minute shoppers rushing by. Was something the matter? Perhaps it was something to do with her father.

What kind of animal created such fear in his own daughter? This morning she had been up at some ungodly hour, looking tired and tense, and had barely spoken to him before she had bolted up to the library, insisting she had work to do. Later on, when he had returned from his run, he had found a note from her informing him she had decided to work in the British Library and wishing him a happy Christmas.

And he had got to wondering what her Christmas would be like.

How was he supposed to walk away from her, knowing she would be all alone for Christmas, especially after witnessing her distress last night?

Coming back inside, she handed her black padded jacket to the waiter and, putting her phone on the table, dropped down to her seat opposite him with a sigh.

Wearing a black and white T-shirt with the logo *TOMBOY* emblazoned on it, she gave him an apologetic smile. 'Sorry. That was my mum. I didn't want to miss her call. I knew that she was driving to my aunt's house today and she's a nervous driver, so I wanted to make sure she got there okay.' She let out another sigh. 'Although now I wish I hadn't: she wants me to go back to Ireland for Christmas.' On the table her phone pinged. She glanced at it before dropping it into her handbag at the side of the table. She rolled her eyes. 'I'm now going to get a barrage of calls and texts from her. My mum thinks I'm nine, not twenty-nine.'

'Why does she want you to go home?'

She hesitated for a moment before admitting, 'I made the stupid mistake of telling her that I saw my father last night.'

What was she not telling him? Why was her mother so concerned? His own concern had him ask sharply, 'Is your father a danger to you?'

She blinked, rightly taken aback by his tone.

He raised his hands in apology. 'Sorry,' he placed his hands on the table between them, 'I can't get out of my mind just how terrified you were last night. It's not right.'

She studied his hands for a moment and then briefly she touched her fingertips against his. 'Thanks for being concerned.' Her eyes held his; there was a flash of uncertainty, deep vulnerability, in her expression, but then, sitting back in her seat, her expression once again closed to scrutiny, she gave a shrug. 'My father isn't a danger to me. My mum was never happy about me spending Christmas alone in the first place. It's the first time we haven't spent Christmas week together—I've tried to get out of it other years but she's very good at persuading me into spending it with her family. God, it's a nightmare—too many people, too many presents to be bought and exchanged, too much food and too much singing.'

'It sounds like fun to me.'

She laughed at that. 'I'm guessing any party is fun to you.' Then, her expression growing quizzical, she said, 'Your life, it seems so busy. You seem to be in a different country every week, hanging out with a different crowd. That constant travel, racing and socialising would exhaust me. Do you ever just long for an easier life?'

He raised an eyebrow. How and why did she know what his life looked like?

He watched their waiter place their food on the table—*tajarin* pasta with wild mushrooms for Alice and roasted venison loin for him—before he asked, 'Are you keeping tabs on me?'

Her mouth dropped open. 'Good God, no. My mum is an avid reader of celebrity magazines, and ever since Kara married into your family she thinks it's her duty to keep up with all of your lives. I could equally tell you about Ivo's win in Henley and your father's trip to Canada this autumn. But you leave both of them standing when it comes to coverage in the media—do you ever take time out? Does being so hectic make you happy?'

He laughed at her question but it came out half-heartedly. Under her calm grey-eyed gaze he started to feel undone. No one had ever asked him that question before—if he was happy. And she seemed genuinely intrigued by his lifestyle. Not in a judgemental way, but more as though it was something she really wanted to understand about him. But how could he explain the restlessness inside of him to her? The need for change and novelty and the energy of others? The need to feel alive? How being alone brought demons he didn't want to know about to the fore? He focused on cutting into his venison, anything to break the unnerving way she was studying him, and nodded towards her plate, encouraging her to eat too. 'Your mum will be reading less about me from now on—I'm moving back to Monrosa to take up my royal duties.'

'What about your powerboat career?'

He cleared his throat, the thought of what he was leaving acting like a punch to his heart. 'I promised my father that as soon as I won the Global Series I would return to Monrosa.'

Laying her fork back into her pasta bowl, she said, 'You don't sound very enthusiastic.'

He shrugged. 'It's what I need to do.'

Lifting her fork again, she rolled the pasta on the prongs. 'At least you'll be able to spend time with your family now.'

'As long as my father doesn't try to force me to marry.'

Alice dropped her fork. Damn it, he had forgotten that she knew nothing about how his father had forced Edwin to marry Kara.

'Why on earth would he do that?' she asked.

'Because it's tradition and what's expected of all royals. We're expected to settle down, produce heirs and live happily ever after.'

Alice's head tilted as she studied him. 'And you don't want any of those things?'

He never had this type of conversation. His friendships and past relationships were based on having a good time. Not this type of soul-searching. And despite his better judgement he heard himself admit, 'I don't want to spend my life second-guessing the feelings of someone else for me.'

'I don't understand what you mean by that.'

The need to get up and walk away itched inside of him. He pulled at his shirt collar, his eyes shifting away from hers. *Dio!* It was hot in here. He was about to make a joke of it, but looking her in the eye again, her calm intelligence, had him confess, 'You think that my lifestyle is exhausting...well, I find relationships exhausting. Despite media accounts, I am not a serial dater. I've had a handful of serious relationships but they have never worked out. I get restless in relationships. I don't like the constant worry of what someone else is thinking and feeling. I've now decided it's easier to be alone. And despite my father's wishes, I never intend on marrying.'

She gave a faint smile at that. 'Whatever makes you happy, Luis—that's what's important. We all don't have to follow the same path in life. Even if others can't or refuse to understand and accept that decision.'

Taken aback by the sad resignation in her voice, thinking of her spending the next week alone, he said, 'Maybe your mum is right and you should return to Ireland.'

'Have you not been listening to me? I have my thesis to finish. And right now that's not happening anytime fast.'

'How long have you been working on it?'

She rolled her eyes. 'Three very long years.'

'Maybe you need a break from it for the next few days. Is there anyone in London you could spend time with, just relaxing?'

'No—my best friend, Toni, is the only person I know who lives in London and she's in Australia at the moment. You may have heard of her boyfriend, Dan Ferguson?'

'No.'

Taking her phone from her bag, she said, 'Last year his TV series on Italian history was a major hit.' She showed him the screen of her phone. On it, a tall blond-haired man wearing dark-framed glasses was surrounded by a large group of beaming women, his expression one of utter bafflement. 'He's especially a huge hit with female fans. Apparently they all love his geeky look. Toni thinks it's hilarious. Her awkward and shy boyfriend a sex symbol.'

He studied the photo. Suddenly not too keen on Dan Ferguson. 'Do you think he's a sex symbol?'

She laughed at that, her eyes dancing with merriment. 'Dan? No! God, no!' Then, pausing, she looked at him with bewilderment.

He cleared his throat. 'Is there anyone waiting for you back in Dublin, a boyfriend?'

She pushed her pasta bowl away. She had barely touched it but suddenly she had lost her appetite. Would Luis stop staring at her so intently? Did he somehow know, detect something in her? She tried not to redden. It was no one's business what her relationship history was like and the decisions she had taken, but she could never shake off the dread for being judged for it. Even by a guy who had admitted to not being particularly good at relationships himself. 'No.'

For the longest while Luis studied her across the table. She felt herself grow even more scarlet. He would laugh. She knew he would. Of course, one of the world's most eligible bachelors, a sophisticated prince, a champion sportsman, a man who had dated some of the most beautiful women in the world, would be amused to know that she was still a virgin.

'Let's go for a walk.'

She glanced down at his half-eaten plate of food. 'What about your lunch?'

Not answering her, he motioned to the maître d', who, after a quick conversation with Luis in Spanish, reappeared with their bill. Luis refused to allow her to pay for the lunch or even pay for her share.

Outside, they walked back in the direction of the British Library. From every shop doorway came the sound of cheerful Christmas songs.

At the entrance to Regent's Park he said he knew a shortcut to the library. The park was quiet but for some runners and families all bundled up in rain gear for yet more forecasted heavy rain later in the day.

'I'm guessing we have messy relationship histories in common?'

She shrugged at his question. 'I wouldn't say so.' She should change the conversation but for some reason the need to tell Luis the truth burned inside her. Why, she couldn't understand. But there had been something in their kiss, something in his care last night, and in all of those awkward moments when their eyes locked and neither of them seemed capable of looking away, that had her add, 'You have histories, I don't.'

Under a towering bare-branched oak, he pulled her to a stop. 'What do you mean…you must have *some* relationship history?'

Did he have to sound so surprised? She tried not to wince and decided to try to laugh it all off. 'I don't think I can count my one and only very brief relationship, as it was so long ago. I was nineteen and it only lasted a year and even at that we lived in different cities, as he was away at university. But, trust me, it confirmed my belief that I'm better out of relationships. He said that I made him unhappy. And I guess I did—he wanted more from the relationship than I could ever give. And with the benefit of hindsight I can see that he wasn't good for me—he wasn't the most patient of people.'

Over his white shirt he was wearing a heavy woollen coat, the seam of the collar done in dark bronze thread. She stared at the collar and the tanned skin of his neck. Evening shadow was already there. No wonder he had grown a beard. The effort of keeping clean-shaven must be a tiresome daily battle. But she preferred him clean-shaven. Preferred seeing the sharp, clean edge of his jawline. This was new to her.

Not once before had she been drawn to a man like this.

'And you haven't been in a relationship since?'

Heat flamed in her belly at the soft tone of his voice.

She swallowed hard. Fell into the beauty of his eyes. Deep, deep green with flecks of brown. 'No.'

He tilted his head, shifted his body to stand even closer to her. 'Why?'

They were alone on the tree-lined path, the day darkening around them. When other people asked her that question she always told them that she was too busy with her studies, that she was perfectly content on her own. But with Luis she wanted to tell him the truth, especially after last night. 'After my dad, I never want to be dependent on someone else.'

His hand touched her jaw. 'I guess we do have that in common—an aversion to relationships.'

His head tilted closer. Her head spun. His nose came close to touching hers. His hand on her jawline was warm and gentle. Seconds passed. His eyes held hers.

Kiss me! Kiss me before I pass out. I know I should walk away. I have work to do and you have a flight to catch. But would one more kiss matter? We wouldn't see each other again for a very long time.

What was he waiting for? She wasn't experienced when it came to men but surely the way his pupils were enlarged meant he was feeling the same pull of desire? Was she going to have to kiss him…again?

She shifted onto her toes. Their noses touched.

His gaze darkened. Her heart pounded in her ears.

Before you go, kiss me one more time. I want to soar, to feel alive.

His mouth brushed against hers. She felt faint with the need for more.

She almost cried out when he pulled back way too soon.

He raked a hand through his hair, his mouth tense. 'I'm staying in London with you for Christmas.'

CHAPTER FOUR

ALICE LET OUT an impatient breath. The house on Fitzalen Square was ablaze with lights, so she took it that Luis was still at home. She had hoped that he would have already left for the dinner party he had invited her to earlier by text message. She had messaged back saying she couldn't go with him. In return he had sent her a video clip from an old black and white movie, of a guy standing outside a department store, impeccably dressed and carrying a bunch of flowers, looking comically hangdog and forlorn as he realised that his date wasn't turning up. Despite her pledge after his shock announcement that he was staying in London for Christmas that she was going to do her best to ignore his presence and the knots he was tying her up into, she had laughed long and hard at the video, earning herself stern looks from her fellow readers in the library.

Why couldn't he have gone home to Monrosa? It would have made her life a whole lot easier. She needed peace and solitude. She wasn't able to figure him out. Why was he really staying in London? He claimed it was to keep her company, but why would someone forgo their Christmas to spend it with a stranger? What was he up to?

Turning, she studied the small park behind her at the centre of Fitzalen Square, which had been transformed for the festive period into Christmas Central. Beneath a huge Christmas tree a temporary stage was playing host to a gospel group who were entertaining a large audience. To the rear of the central fountain, a Christmas market was busy with shoppers now that the earlier heavy rain had given way to a crisp, clear night sky.

She shuddered as the choir broke into a popular Christmas song. Her dad had used to sing it in the car. She glanced back at the house. And then at her phone. It was close to eight. Luis must be leaving for his dinner party soon.

Bracing herself, she entered the park, deciding to take refuge in the Christmas market. She would find a stall selling coffee and buy a triple espresso. She had a long night of writing ahead of herself.

Head down, she ignored the stalls, but from the corner of her eye she spotted handcrafted baubles and a stall selling pine wreaths with enormous red bows. She came to a stop, intrigued, when a little boy exclaimed in delight at a stall laden down with a ceramic Christmas village snow scene that featured the most exquisite crafted churches and houses and miniature people and animals straight out of an Alpine village. Bending down, she gazed into the window of a wooden cabin, smiling at the scene inside of a family hanging Christmas stockings, the youngest child hanging both hers and that of the family dog, who was seated at her side. When the stall owner asked her if she wanted some help, she shook her head and backed away.

The food stalls were all placed to the rear of the market. She groaned to see a long line at the stand selling hot beverages. She eyed a couple walking away from the stall, both of them laughing in delight at the huge dollop of cream and chocolate shavings on top of their hot chocolates. Her stomach growled. And she turned away when the couple stopped and kissed, laughter and happiness shining in their eyes.

A few stalls down there was a doughnut stand. She hesitated for a moment but then marched up to it. Stood in line. Ordered one doughnut but then changed her mind and ordered three. Well, it was a three-for-the-price-of-two offer after all.

She found a bench, not as far away from everyone else as she would have liked, but it was the best she could do and, sitting down, she bit into the doughnut. She closed her eyes as the sugar melted in her mouth. She took a second bite, opened her eyes, but almost choked when she tried to swallow. Luis was walking in her direction, eyeing her half-eaten doughnut hungrily. Could she find any peace in this world?

With a grin he sat beside her.

She passed the box of doughnuts over and he picked one out.

She wanted to ask him why he wasn't dressed for a dinner party but thought better of it. Instead she nodded towards the box. 'I reckoned I need some sugar before I get back to my writing. I'm going to have to work until past midnight at least.'

He raised an eyebrow, studying her way too closely for her liking. Why did he look at her that way and yet when she virtually offered herself on a plate earlier he had backed away from really kissing her? She was useless at all of this. She didn't understand flirting...was she reading all of his signals wrong? The best policy for the next few days was avoidance—at least that way she wouldn't make a fool of herself. Again.

She jumped up. Put her half-eaten doughnut back into the box and tossed the box into her already heaving handbag, squishing it next to her laptop and notes. 'Talking of work, I'd better go and do some. Enjoy your evening out.'

Luis nodded, but instead of staying where he was as she had hoped he would he stood and began to walk with her, back towards the pedestrian gate opposite the house. 'I'm not going out. I said that I was staying in London to support you. And I meant that. I'll stay in and cook you dinner while you work.'

'There's no need...' She paused in her protest, realising it was futile, given that the recipient had decided to wander off to a stall where two surly-looking teenagers were glaring out at the world. All of the other shoppers were wisely giving their stall a wide berth.

Luis smiled at the teenagers, who were selling dark blue football jerseys.

In unison they folded their arms, their glares intensifying even more when he lifted up a rain-soaked jersey. She guessed that at one point the jersey would have had the same logo as that printed on a display football at the side of the stall—*Our Place FC*—but some of the adhesive letters had lifted off the jersey and now it just read *Our lace*.

The boy wearing a bobble hat nodded at the jersey, his scowl deepening. 'We didn't know it was going to rain. No one warned us.' He stared at Luis as though it were Luis's fault that the heavens had decided to open that afternoon, and added, 'We've tried getting in contact with the supplier for a refund but there's no telephone number on the website and he's not answering our emails. My mum says we've been had.'

Luis nodded. 'Bad luck.'

The other boy, who was wearing a bottle-green parka jacket, gave an angry laugh. 'You can jog on now, mate. There's nothing for you to buy here. We're only here because my mum won't let us go home. She said she didn't waste all that time convincing someone to allow us to have a stall for us to leave on our first day.'

Luis picked up the football, bounced it on the ground and did some impressive solos. Alice rolled her eyes. Was there anything this man couldn't do?

'So where's *"Our Place"* located?' Luis asked as he flicked the ball towards the boy with the hat.

The boy caught it, his scowl for a moment replaced with an awestruck expression at Luis's skills. 'There's an empty field behind our flats... we're trying to get a team together from the neighbourhood. There's no local team. And the kids are bored.' Remembering the rain-soaked jerseys, the boy picked up one, his expression one of disgust, before flinging it back down on the table. 'We need to raise money for goalposts. We had hoped to sell these jerseys.'

Luis nodded. Considered the two boys for a moment and then gestured to the entire table. 'I'll buy everything.'

The two boys looked at him as though he had lost his mind. The guy in the parka said, 'All of the jerseys are destroyed.'

Luis shrugged and then smiled in her direction. 'I'll take two, one for myself and my friend Alice. Who knows, we might come along and watch you play some time?' Pausing to take business cards from his wallet, he passed one to each boy, along with a healthy number of banknotes, 'I trust this will adequately cover my bill? Take the rest of the jerseys home and see if they can be rescued. If they can, hand them out to local children and encourage them to join the club.'

They walked away from the speechless boys.

He called me his friend.

She eyed him warily, more confused than ever as to what to make of him.

Are we friends? I suppose I should be pleased that that's how he sees things...that's way safer than there being more to this. Two friends sharing a house over Christmas. Nothing complicated or worth spending time fretting over. Friends who just might meet up again in the future if they happen to cross paths.

As they neared the gate out of the park, the boy wearing the green parka raced after them. Fist pumping Luis, his eyes aglow, the boy then gave Luis an awkward hug before running away, giving a whoop.

Luis laughed, his eyes shining with pleasure. This she did not expect from him—other people had given the boys a wide berth, but not Luis. What was it in him that had seen their story, their disappointment masked by belligerence? He had an innate intuition and kindness that was so at odds with his public wild and carefree image.

Inside the house, she followed him down to the basement. 'That was an incredibly nice thing to do.'

Shrugging, he went into the utility room and deftly loaded the wet jerseys into the washing machine, popping in some detergent and putting the machine onto a wash cycle. Turning, he raised an eyebrow. 'I'm not sure if the jerseys will survive a wash, but it's worth a go.'

She eyed the washing machine and then him. 'You wash your own clothes?'

He laughed at that. 'Why shouldn't I?'

She followed him back up to the sitting room, where he used a remote control to switch on the lights of the Christmas tree that was sitting in the bay window. 'You could have just bought a few jerseys from the boys—why buy everything?'

Moving to twist around a decoration of a girl on skis that was facing backwards, he answered, 'They reminded me of myself when I was a teenager.'

She stood in front of him. The white lights of the tree flashed against his dark skin like snowflakes. 'Really? I thought you were born smiling.'

'I went through a long and protracted teenage rebellion. It was only when I found powerboating that I changed. It gave me a sense of purpose. Something to aim towards.'

She caught the emotion in his voice—was it regret? 'And now that you're leaving that career—it must be difficult?'

He stepped back from the tree. Unbuttoned his grey wool coat. Unwound his dark grey and cream scarf from around his neck. 'Resuming my royal duties is what I have to do.'

She raised an eyebrow at his unenthusiastic tone.

He yanked off his coat, ran a hand against his neck. Rocked on his heels for a moment, eyeing her all the while. 'Come to dinner with me. I have been hearing great things about the new restaurant in Hotel Russo. I need to get out.'

She went to say no but he interrupted her as though guessing what she was about to say. 'It's two days before Christmas. We should be celebrating. Not stuck inside.' He moved away, his restlessness clear. 'Come on, Alice. It's only dinner. You can work tomorrow. I'm a terrible chef—you really don't want to have to eat whatever I manage to cook for you tonight.'

She wavered for a moment. Swayed by his eagerness but even more so by his kindness towards the boys. He waited for her answer with a forced patience. And she remembered his soft gentleness with her last night. How could she turn him down? But she had to at least make an attempt to call a halt to how he was throwing her completely off schedule. 'Why not go to the dinner party you were invited to?'

He stopped and considered that for a moment. And then with a hint of bewilderment, as though something was just dawning on him, he answered, 'I guess I'd much rather spend time with you.'

She blushed, smiled, felt rather faint at the softness of his voice, at the way he was concentrating on her with one hundred per cent focus. It would be so easy to fall for every word he said. She needed to tread carefully. No, scratch that: she needed to take this man and any notions he fostered in her down with a sledgehammer. She folded her arms and tilted her chin to deliver one of her best unimpressed stares. 'That's not true—what are you up to, Luis?'

He laughed. Long and deep. His eyes sparkling with amusement. His laughter wrapped around her, and despite herself she smiled, taking far too much pleasure in being able to create that happiness in him. He eventually controlled himself enough to say, 'I like chatting with you. Your crankiness is refreshing.'

With that he tilted his head, those eyes of his watching her, softly appealing to her to accept his invite.

She rolled her eyes. Let out an irritated breath. 'How can a girl possibly say no to such flattery?' She turned for the door. 'I'm warning you though, once tonight is over, I'm one hundred per cent focused on my thesis.' She stopped at the doorway, adding, 'After tonight I don't want to be disturbed...or reminded that it's Christmas. Is that a deal?'

He sauntered over to her. She waited for him to say yes. But instead, his voice disturbingly intense, a dangerous heat in his eyes, he said, 'I'll try...but do you really want me to stay away?'

She knew she should give him a sharp retort, but her throat was suddenly dry. All she could muster up was a weak smile, her pulse pounding in her ears, the memory of their kiss in the palace garden, the heat of his mouth, the beauty, the rightness of his touch, his scent, leaving her with no option but to walk away from him now without an answer, her skin flaming with the knowledge that he watched her every single shaky step as she climbed the stairs.

Following Alice as the maître d' led them to their table in the dimly lit restaurant, Luis tried not to stare at the curve of Alice's bottom encased in soft black leather. She had removed her coat to reveal a cream open-neck silk blouse tucked inside a black leather mini-skirt. He wanted so much more with her. He wanted to kiss her again and experience that heart-jolting, addictive hunger her mouth, her taste, the feel of her skin against his had stirred in him. He wanted to move beyond that tough exterior she presented to the world and know her better.

But to do so would be selfish. How would getting entangled with him help her in any way? *And* she was practically family, so that was another reason he needed to draw a line in the nature of their relationship—he'd allow himself some light flirting, he was only human, after all, but ultimately the next few days were about Alice not having to spend Christmas alone.

He took his seat opposite her at their table, which was placed next to the floor-to-ceiling glass window that spanned the entire length of the restaurant located on the top floor of the hotel. The candle on their table flickered in the window's reflection and he smiled when Alice placed her hands against the glass and peered out. 'I can just about see the Thames—the view from here must be spectacular during the day.' She let out a disappointed sigh. 'It's a shame it's so hard to see anything at night.'

Their waiter, who had come alongside the table, cleared his throat. Alice leapt away from the window.

'We dim the interior lights to allow a better view, but we do have a number of outdoor areas that diners can avail themselves of for their desserts and coffees.' Pausing to glance in his direction, the waiter added, 'Usually they are booked in advance, but I can organise for an area to be reserved for you, Your Highness.'

Across from him Alice squirmed in her seat. He raised an eyebrow in question as to what she thought of the idea of having dessert outside and she nodded with a sheepish smile.

The waiter presented them with their menus and after disappearing for a few minutes returned with water and amuse-bouches and took their orders. They agreed to forgo a starter and head straight for the main course, both of them choosing the restaurant's signature dish of halibut and oysters.

Sitting back in his chair, he nodded towards Alice's reflection in the window. 'Personally, I like the view—I get to see you twice.'

She scowled. He laughed, knowing he enjoyed teasing her way too much but that it was proving to be way too entertaining to stop.

'You mean you enjoy being able to see your own reflection.' She tilted her head, impending revenge glittering in her eyes. 'So, what's it like to be considered one of the most eligible men in the world? That accolade must go to your head.'

'I stopped reading anything about myself a long time ago. Trust me, disassociation from your public image is the best thing anyone in the public eye can do. The person portrayed in the media is not me.' He paused as the waiter brought the glass of Merlot he had ordered and a sparkling water for Alice to the table. When the waiter had left he raised his glass in a toast. 'If you stick around long enough you might actually believe that.'

She considered him for a moment. Her hair was tied up, her long, slender neck seeming even more vulnerable without the weight of her hair. A plain silver chain hung around it, resting in the hollow of her throat. 'So how would you describe yourself?'

'A professional sportsman,' he paused, catching himself, 'or should I say an ex-pro?'

'Are you definitely leaving powerboating?'

He took a drink of his wine; the tannins were smooth, but something caught at the back of his throat. 'I haven't publicly announced it yet...' He trailed off.

'It must be a hard decision, given how successful you were—will you miss it?'

With all my heart.

'Not the losses or the frustration of mechanical problems and bad weather and wrong tactics.'

She studied him with that unnerving quiet perceptiveness of hers that totally unsettled him. She was waiting for him to say something more…she knew he was holding back the truth. He took a drink. Looked to see if there was any sign of their waiter. When would their food arrive? And still she said nothing. The silence was too much. He admitted in a rush, his voice carrying how much he begrudged and felt exposed at doing so, 'I'll miss the sense of purpose, the camaraderie… The team are like a family to me.'

Placing an elbow on the table, a hand cupping her cheek, she said, 'That's a huge amount of things to have to give up.'

He arched his neck, his legs beneath the table restlessly moving with the urge to get up and go, the understanding in her voice, the understanding of what he was leaving behind, too much to handle.

'Tell me about the team. Tell me about what it was like to chase the world championship.'

Surprised by her question, he hesitated for a moment. But then he realised he did want to talk about Justin, Ryan, Anna and the rest of the team and the lows and highs they had endured over their eight-year campaign to become the top team in the world. He told her about them throughout their meal and as their waiter cleared away their dinner plates he realised that, though it was crushing to know that that time in his life was over, having a chance to reminisce about it, to share the highs and lows of all those years with someone, made it just that little bit easier.

'What will your responsibilities be when you return to Monrosa?'

He grimaced at her question. *Dio!* He dreaded the arguments that would come in the New Year as the exact nature of his role was thrashed out. His father no doubt would be as scathing and dismissive of his abilities and commitment to Monrosa as he always was.

Across the table, she waited for his answer with a calm understanding. She knew only too well the dysfunction of families. Was that why he found it so easy…okay, none of this was easy…but was her own past the reason why he was talking about things he had never spoken to another person about before?

'With my father abdicating and Edwin taking over as monarch, my role has not been fully decided. My father when he was mon-

arch had been making noises about me joining the treasury—my degree was in Finance
and Economics...well, it was until I left university early to take up powerboating. I reckon
he thinks I can do least damage there, hidden
out of public view and under the careful watch
of his close ally, the Chancellor.'

'But now that Edwin has taken over, if powerboating is so important to you, why can't
you—?'

He interrupted her, knowing where this conversation was going, 'I'm not going back on
my promise that I would return to Monrosa.
Edwin has ambitious plans for it and is looking
for my support. Which I unquestionably will
give him, even if it means joining the treasury
to appease my father—I'm sure it will be more
fun than it sounds.'

'That's very honourable...' Pausing, she bit
her lip, cleared her throat. 'I admire you for
keeping your word...so many people promise
things and never follow up on them. But can
there be a compromise? Can you have a role
where you can use all your experience in sport?
And, though I'll admit to not being the best
judge of character, to me you have the most incredible people skills. People gravitate towards
you. You should be in a role that inspires oth-

ers, not be stuck behind a desk. Look at how well you dealt with the boys this evening in the park. You're a leader, a role model, a mentor; use those skills.'

He took a drink of water, trying to process everything she had said. Her passion, her conviction, her assessment of him, throwing him.

Was that who he was?

But no—he was the dissident of the family, the one who caused the trouble, the one who constantly locked horns with their father. A brother who put socialising and winning above the needs of his siblings. Wanting any excuse not to have to acknowledge all that was wrong in his family. He had walked away from them—not wanting to have to deal with his father's bitterness, Edwin's pointless attempts to keep their father appeased and Ivo's complete withdrawal from them all.

Leaning further into the table, she placed both arms on the white linen cloth. 'Kara rang me earlier; she's disappointed you won't be in Monrosa for Christmas.'

'Trust me, I know. Edwin has made that perfectly clear.'

For long moments she eyed him and then, pushing back into her chair, she folded her arms and said quietly, 'You're not staying in London just for my sake, are you? It's an excuse not to go home, isn't it?'

For a split second he was going to argue that she was wrong. Hating to be called out, suddenly feeling like a cad. He closed his eyes for a moment and then, opening them, admitted, 'Wanting to help you was my primary reasoning…but I will admit that it was a convenient excuse not to spend Christmas in Monrosa too.'

'At least you admitted it…' She bit her lip and stared towards their reflections, a deep heat colouring her cheeks. 'My father used to play mind games with me…' yet another deep inhale was followed by a shrug, and then she looked at him. 'Promise me you won't do the same. Promise me you'll always be honest with me.'

The simplicity of her words but the emotion behind them, the depth to them, the endless possible implications of them, left him momentarily bowled over. His heart was racing for reasons he couldn't comprehend and on a shaky exhale he reached his hand across the table. 'I promise.'

Ever so slowly she laid her hand in his.

They smiled at one another. An unsure but intimate smile. That felt as through every certainty he believed in was being pulled right from underneath him.

CHAPTER FIVE

ALREADY PRETTY SHAKEN by the unexpected powerful intimacy of her conversation with Luis, Alice stared in disbelief when their waiter led them to their outdoor space that was positioned in the seclusion of a small upper terrace on the restaurant roof.

What had she got herself into?

The waiter had promised them views and yes, there they were—the Thames and all the stunning iconic buildings that lay along her meandering path through London—but what he had failed to mention was that instead of sitting at a table they were going to have dessert whilst lying on a double daybed. And he had also failed to mention that they would be all alone up here.

'We can go back downstairs if you prefer,' Luis said.

Was her dismay that obvious?

For crying out loud, Alice, it's a daybed. You're both fully clothed and wearing heavy overcoats. Relax and enjoy yourself... How many times in your life will you get to lie next to a real-life prince in one of the most beautiful cities in the world? At least now, for once, you'll have a story that will beat Toni's exploits as the partner of a reluctant celebrity.

Grabbing the cream and green striped woollen blanket at the bottom of the bed, she stepped out of her high heels and tried to lie down as gracefully as that manoeuvre would allow, trying to ignore his amusement.

The rear of the bed was propped up, so after offering him a share of the blanket, which he refused, as she had hoped he would do, she tucked her legs beneath her, anchoring the blanket under her bare feet.

Settling in, she closed her eyes, the distant traffic, the heat from the overhead outdoor heaters all surprisingly soothing. She tried to focus on her breathing…and not on Luis lying next to her, the way the mattress sagged at his movement, his arm brushing against hers. She shifted away. Breathed deeply into her lungs.

Silence followed. She opened her eyes and let them wander in his direction. He was looking at her. She smiled. Feeling unaccountably shy.

He smiled back.

'Are you sure you were a sullen teenager? I can't imagine you being one, given your perpetual sunny nature,' she said.

He raised an eyebrow. Unbuttoning his coat and then his navy suit jacket, he yanked his white shirt out of the waistband of his trousers and, lifting it up, revealed a small tattoo beside his ribs.

She edged closer to see it, unconsciously touching a fingertip against the beauty of the tree tattooed on his golden skin—the powerful trunk giving way to soaring green branches.

Seconds passed. Her finger lingered on the warmth of his skin. She knew she should pull away but something kept it there. She tried to ignore the tight awareness in the air between them. 'I don't think something this beautiful can be classed as rebellion.'

He laughed. Caught hold of her finger, mischief glittering in his eyes. 'It can if you're a fifteen-year-old royal. Show me your tattoo.'

'I don't have one.'

'What a surprise. I take it you were a model teenager.'

She laughed at the fact that he had rightly guessed her clean-cut teenage years. But then, sobering, she admitted, a lump in her throat,

'My mum had enough to contend with without me going off the rails.'

He grimaced, lowering their hands to the mattress but not letting go of her finger. 'I'm sorry.'

She shrugged, wanting the hole that had opened up inside herself in remembering how haunted, how fragile her mum had been during her teenage years to disappear. 'It's okay.' Taking her hand away from his, she pretend-frowned, wanting to keep this conversation light. 'Why a tree? Most teenagers go for something dark, like a skull. A flourishing tree doesn't exactly represent teenage rebellion.'

Luis tucked his shirt back in and fastened his jacket button. 'It's on my mother's family crest.'

She grimaced. 'Now it's my turn to say sorry.'

He went to speak. Stopped. And then gently said, 'Sometimes I struggle to picture her, to remember her voice.'

'It wasn't fair that you lost her at such a young age... I still remember hearing about her death on the radio, I was in the car with my mum. The newsreader listed your ages, Luis was the same age as me—we were both only ten.' Pausing, she rested her hand on his arm before admitting, 'I remember crying, thinking about you all losing your mum and how terrible that must be.'

For a moment his hand rested again on hers. And she stopped breathing at the hint of a grateful smile that lifted ever so slightly on his mouth. But at the sound of approaching footsteps he moved away.

Their waiter placed their desserts on the tables on either side of the bed.

She grinned at her chocolate mousse tower that had a disc of chocolate on top. Lifting the disc, she bit into it. 'I adore chocolate.'

He laughed. 'So I gathered, given the state of that tin of chocolates last night.'

Lifting her plate, she cut into the mousse tower. 'If you'd had the day I had yesterday, you'd have eaten them too.'

'I hope you're not talking about my arrival?' he asked with a grin, lifting out a spoon of his crème brûlée.

'Well… I have to admit, your arrival was unexpected… Kara had promised me that the house would be empty.'

'It's surprising that we never met before Kara's wedding—she's mentioned you a lot over the years.'

'I'd intended on visiting her but work always came in the way. And then things got awkward when I moved in with her dad.' Seeing his quizzical look, she explained, 'After I left school, I stayed working locally—I wasn't sure what I wanted to do, and I didn't want to leave my mum. We had only moved to the town a few years previously and she didn't know that many people. She struggled with panic attacks after she left my dad. One of the jobs I had was as a tour guide in the town's Norman castle. I fell in love with history, thanks to that experience, and when my mum was well enough I went to university. I was twenty-two. I couldn't afford any accommodation in Dublin so I moved in with Kara's dad. But it wasn't just because I was penniless—all of the family were worried about him.' Placing her dessert back on her side table, her heart suddenly sore with emotion, she admitted, 'Kara's brother, Michael, you know...'

'Yes. I know he died...' he paused, his expression one of utter kindness and understanding, 'and that he took his own life.'

'It was such a shock. He and Kara used to spend their summer holidays with us at my Aunt Nina's house. We had been close—we grew apart as teenagers, but I have such lovely memories of Michael sitting on Cloghroe beach, reading his book or telling us over dinner some obscure fact. It was only in later years that I realised he used to make some of them up—he had once convinced us that Sir Walter Raleigh had stopped in Cloghroe Bay and was seen by locals burying something on the beach. All of us cousins spent the entire summer digging up the beach, which of course suited him perfectly, as we were too busy to pester him to play with us. He must have thought we were daft to believe him—but to us he was our cool older cousin who could do no wrong.'

Luis gave her a sympathetic smile. 'Kara doesn't talk about him a lot—I think she finds it too hard—but I know she misses him terribly.'

'After his death and then Kara's parents' divorce, my mum and her sisters were worried about her dad—they asked me to move in to keep an eye on him. Thankfully we got on really well. But I could see how low he was; if I hadn't already been turned off marriage, seeing how destroyed he was by the divorce would definitely have convinced me that nothing is worth that heartache. I thought Kara felt the same way about marriage—the few times we talked about relationships over the past few years she had hinted as much. But now she's happily married to Edwin.' Pausing, she waited for him to say something, to join in with her amazement over Edwin's and Kara's surprise marriage, but when he didn't she added, 'Did they send you their Christmas card? I usually just put any I get into a drawer, not wanting to be reminded that it's that time of year again. But even I felt compelled to display their card on my mantelpiece—it's so good to see Kara happy. How it happened I'll never understand— what do you think changed between them?'

Dio! What was he supposed to say? Just a little while ago she had asked him to always be honest with her. But would he be betraying Edwin and Kara by telling her of their wedding secret? Could he trust Alice not to tell anyone else? She was waiting for his answer, her expectant expression turning puzzled and then suspicious. Why was he even hesitating?

Because Edwin's and Kara's trust and closeness, how they are both blossoming as people within their marriage, the power of their togetherness, mocks everything you like to believe about love.

'Their marriage…at first it was not as it seemed.'

'What do you mean?'

'My father changed the law of succession—

for Edwin to succeed to the throne he had to marry.'

Alice's mouth dropped open. 'You are kidding me.' Then, her brows slamming together, she demanded, 'Are you saying Edwin convinced Kara into a sham marriage?'

'Don't get mad with me. I was totally against the idea at the time. I thought they were both crazy.'

She shook her head. 'What? And now you agree with it? Knowing everything Kara has been through?'

He shrugged. 'They're in love—or so they claim. They have both admitted to being in love with one another for years, but after Michael died everything became complicated.'

Alice made a disbelieving snort. 'I can't believe Edwin persuaded her…honestly, what was Kara thinking of?'

Last month Edwin and Kara had travelled to watch him take part in his penultimate race in Corsica. It had been sickening…and kind of enviable just how in love they had been with each other—constantly touching, sharing looks and intimate smiles when they thought nobody was looking. 'But if they're happy now—isn't that what's important?'

'I guess,' she answered with a disgruntled expression.

'You're not jealous, are you?'

'No! Obviously. Why would I be jealous of something I don't want?' Slamming her arms together, she stared at him suspiciously. 'Why, are you changing your mind about not wanting to marry?'

He gave a shiver. 'No.' But then his gaze caught hold of hers and something unaccountable broke apart inside of him. And without any thought or sense he heard himself say, 'To have someone close, it must be...' Coming to an abrupt halt at her appalled expression, he scrambled to change the subject away from himself. 'So if marriage isn't on the cards for you, what are your dreams for the future?'

For long seconds she considered him but then with a sigh she answered, 'Up to a few months ago I was certain as to what I wanted—to finish my PhD and get a full-time lecturing position—but I'm not sure any more. I just can't find the motivation to finish my thesis—and that must say something. Sometimes I wonder if I was wrong to start a history degree in the first place.'

'It sounds to me as though you need a break away from writing.'

Shifting back to rest against the daybed, she answered, 'Maybe you're right.' For a while she looked up towards the night sky and then back to him. 'What about you—what are your dreams?'

'I've just achieved it—to win the global series.'

'You must have others.'

'Not particularly.'

Alice considered him with a puzzled expression. 'I had you pegged as someone who always had something else to achieve, some other grand plan. Uber-positive about everything in your life.'

He shrugged, trying not to give away how much he hated how she was pinpointing all that was wrong in his life right now. He was rudderless. Without an identity. A purpose in life. 'Positivity is my defence shield.'

'Does it work?'

He laughed. 'Most of the time, but with you it seems to fade.'

She laughed and then, sobering, she said, 'Okay, I'm going to admit that I don't know what you mean by that, and whether you're pointing out a flaw in my personality.'

She had asked for his honesty. He pulled in a breath, doubt and uncertainty tightening his chest at the wisdom of this conversation. 'I manage to hide what's really inside of myself from others…but not with you.'

Alice grimaced. 'I'm sorry—I don't mean to ask so many questions…it just seems right with you.'

He nodded. He understood what she meant—neither of them was looking for what was happening between them, neither of them wanted this depth of understanding and attraction.

He edged a little closer to her. His arm against hers, inches separating their heads, which were resting against the pillows. The silver in her eyes glittered. Her cheekbones reddened. Her full lips parted ever so slightly. *Dio!* But she was beautiful. 'Just make sure that you don't hurt me.'

'Me hurt you?' she asked in a low whisper.

He moved even closer. 'Well, you did kiss me.' He paused, remembering his initial doubts that soon transformed into a wave of physical pleasure and chemistry. He contemplated her lips, their wide, full shape. The night of Edwin's wedding she had left traces of her lipstick on his mouth. 'And then you ran away. I was left wondering what I had done wrong.'

She let out a tiny sigh of disbelief. 'Trust me, you didn't do anything wrong.'

He touched his hand against her jawline. Desire zapped through his body, the urge to kiss her and a whole lot more tingled in every nerve ending. 'Prove it—kiss me and this time don't run away.'

She smiled but quickly realised he was being deadly serious. She hesitated for a moment but then moved towards him, until inches separated them. He could feel her breath on his cheek, the light scent of her perfume. His own anticipation and desire were reflected in the silver pools of her eyes. Her lips found him, tentative and soft. And then everything went crazy. Her mouth opened. He heard her sigh. Her hand was on his neck. Pulling him closer. Lost to the power of the kiss, he went with her when she pulled him down the bed, so that they were both lying flat. She unbuttoned his coat and then his jacket, her hand hot over the cotton of his shirt. A charge went through him to feel her thumb move against his ribcage in small, rhythmic movements as though she wanted to caress his soul. His hand wound around the soft, silky length of her hair, loving the warmth of her mouth, the smoothness of her skin. His body buzzed with a hot craving that came from the most elemental part of him.

She moaned when he shifted his weight onto

her. Felt her body buckle beneath him. He deepened their kiss, her hand shifting around to run the length of his spine.

He wanted to sleep with her. He wanted to know her body, whip her coat and clothes away. He wanted to taste her skin, cup her breasts in his hands, watch her fall to pieces. Would she scream? What would her favourite position be? He pictured her on top, her hair cascading down around her breasts, her hips moving in a slow dance, his back arching to meet her.

But, this was madness. She didn't need this complication in her life. He dragged himself away from her addictive mouth and rolled onto his side.

She looked at him with a dazed expression, her mouth bruised, heat glowing in her cheeks. But then she bolted up to sitting. 'I… Sorry… that went on longer than I intended,' she gave him a guilty smile, her eyes fleetingly meeting his before she looked away, 'but I can definitely confirm that there's nothing wrong with your kisses.'

She leapt off the bed. 'Well…it's been… lovely. But I guess it's time that we called it a night.' With that, she gestured vaguely in the direction of the stairwell that would take them back to the restaurant and bolted away.

CHAPTER SIX

SHELTERED IN THE safety of the department store entrance, Alice surveyed the mass of humanity sidestepping one another along the length of Oxford Street. The pandemonium of last-minute Christmas Eve shopping. A chaos that was far removed from her usual Christmas shopping, which was always done online, a week before the big day. She refused to be pressured into buying gifts any time earlier than then, hating the frenzied flurry of consumerism the marketing companies loved to create. In a few simple clicks she always bought a spa day for her mum in a local hotel and a book hamper from her local bookshop for each of her extended families. A few simple clicks and her Christmas obligations were over and done with.

She checked her phone. It was close to lunchtime. How was it possible that she had spent three hours shopping? It was as though she had stepped into a time machine when she entered the doors of the famous department store earlier that day. Who knew there were so many things to buy…? And yet it had proved near impossible to find anything appropriate.

Adjusting the shopping bags in her hands, she frowned and wondered what Luis would make of the presents she had eventually bought. He was probably used to receiving scarily expensive presents—would he find hers laughable? Should she just return them? She glanced back into the store. The queues at the tills were even longer than when she had waited in line to pay. There was no way she was going back in there. Bracing herself to step out into the stream of shoppers rushing by, she caught the eye of an older man waiting by the doorway. He looked as unimpressed with this shopping malarkey as she was. She did an eye roll to her fellow sufferer and said, 'It'll be all over by tomorrow thankfully…bar the arguing, of course.'

The man frowned and in fairness to him attempted to laugh along with her, but then he backed towards the door and fled inside, obviously preferring the madness that lay within to having to converse with a crazy lady outside.

What should she do now? Well, the obvious answer was to get herself back to Fitzalen

Square and her thesis. But that meant having to see Luis. And after last night she just knew that she would blush and be all awkward and she didn't want to give him that satisfaction.

She really hadn't meant for their kiss to get so hot and heavy. If he hadn't rolled away…but he had. And now she was mortified. She had been up at six this morning. Determined to work. But after two hours of fidgeting, and rewriting the same paragraph over and over again, she had thrown in the towel and decided to escape the house before Luis climbed out of bed to postpone her embarrassment a little longer. But before she headed out into the misty morning she had gone to her bedroom to fetch a jumper and spotted all her Christmas presents her mum had insisted she bring with her to London. And it had dawned on her that Luis would probably have no presents to open tomorrow. All because he had decided to stay in London and keep her company. For a few moments she had toyed with the idea of sharing her presents with him, but, given what her mum and aunties had gifted her in previous years, she reckoned that Luis wasn't in need of an assortment of girly shower gels and body creams.

Now, bracing herself, she stepped onto the

footpath and was quickly swept along by the human train of shoppers. But when, for the fifth time in as many minutes, she ran into the back of someone who decided now was a good time to check their phone, she diverted off onto a side street. It would take her longer to get home—but, as much as it pained her to admit it, she was happy to find any old excuse to avoid the dual taunts in her life right now— her thesis and Luis.

The side street was lined with restaurants and cafés. In spite of the rain-laden skies, shoppers had bravely opted to sit outside. And, instead of fretting about the weather, the groups of families, friends and couples all seemed buoyed up by the season, their laughter deep and excitement shining in their eyes.

Ahead of her, a little girl dressed in a knee-length red wool coat with white fur trim broke away from her mother and raced along the footpath to a man who swept her up into his arms, kissing her forehead and then embracing the woman, all three of them forming a tight hug that cocooned them into a huddle of love and giggles.

She crossed the road. Walked by a Belgian-chocolate shop, the gold interior of the store shining out into the greyness of the day like a beacon. She came to a stop, spun around and went inside, and bought herself a family-size milk chocolate and hazelnut bar.

She found a street bench. Dropped herself and her bags onto it heavily. Yanked the wrapper from the bar. Ate a square. And then another. It was hard to swallow. But she was ravenous. She squeezed her eyes shut. She was *not* going to cry out here in public.

What was the matter with her?

I'm just overwhelmed by my thesis. I'm in a strange city. And I'm missing my mum. That's all.

No, Alice. You're lonely.

She bit down on another square of chocolate, trying to tune out the voice in her head.

Let's face it. You're lonely. And spending time with Luis is driving that fact home. It's all very well living in your lovely bubble in Dublin, where work and studying distract you from every emotion inside you, but Luis is shining an unwelcome light on everything you want to pretend isn't wrong in your life. You didn't leave the house this morning because you were embarrassed by last night—you left because you were so desperate to see him again this morning. And that terrified you.

Tossing the chocolate bar into her handbag, she grabbed the shopping bags, her heart pounding. She tried to stand, but her legs wouldn't cooperate.

She really liked Luis. She *really, really* liked him.

And not just in a *you make me weak* type of way. That, she could handle. Not that she'd admit it to anyone, but she was given to crushes. She'd had a long-running one on a guy who came into the café every morning. After two long years he had asked her out. But they hadn't got beyond their first date. How hadn't she ever noticed his habit of sucking between his two front teeth in all those years that he had stood at the opposite side of the counter and waited for his Americano?

She didn't just fancy Luis. She actually liked him. Admired him. Thought he was pretty cool, in fact.

What on earth was she going to do with all of this? Get the first flight back to Dublin before she did something stupid? Okay, so she wasn't exactly experienced on the bed front, but she was definitely getting vibes off him that his thoughts towards her weren't one hundred per cent pure.

She smiled at that. Giggled. An elderly woman walking by diverted away from her.

She wanted to call out, *I'm not crazy, hon-*

estly! But decided not to scare the poor lady any further. And anyway, she wasn't certain if she could actually claim to be the picture of sanity. Not when, despite her previous reservations about Luis's character, she was actually picturing them sharing a bed.

Okay, so it was only a fantasy. She would never act upon it. But the fact that she was even dreaming about it was worrying.

She needed to calm down. Remember that Luis would be leaving for Monrosa in two days. She was going to get a grip. Starting now. She stood. Straightened that backbone that had got her through many ups and downs in her life so far. She was going home, where she would greet him with a chilled-out air. And, most important of all, she was going to get back to finishing her PhD.

His feet pounding the footpath, Luis muttered a curse. Rain he could handle but this hail shower was beyond ridiculous. Thoughts of the blue skies he had left behind in the Bahamas mocked him as he rounded a corner, the wind firing the hailstones into him at full force.

If he had stayed in the Bahamas he would now be at Justin's beach house, taking part in his annual beach volleyball tournament or playing chase in the sea with Justin's kids, Flo and Jordi. Not out here, battling the weather and battling his own head.

She was getting to him. And not just because she kissed like an angel…with a few dirty thoughts in mind. Her strength, her vulnerability, her coolness, her sense of humour…they were all burying themselves deep inside him. Despite the hammering hailstones that were pinging off his skin, he chuckled to himself. How had she described his kiss last night? Oh, yeah—'of an adequate standard'.

Ahead in Fitzalen Square the Christmas tree swayed in the near gale. He jogged past some other equally foolhardy people also out in this weather, one of them, hidden beneath an umbrella, valiantly fighting the hail and wind to keep that umbrella upright. A few steps on and said umbrella went sailing by him, thumping against the footpath. He chased after it, passing his own front door in the process. On and on it bumped along the footpath, refusing to allow him to grab hold of it. Eventually its escape was halted by the black wrought-iron railings at the end of the square.

He turned to return it to its owner. And grinned when that owner came running towards him, melting hailstones streaming down her face, shopping bags thumping against her legs. She stood under the shelter of the umbrella and said breathlessly, 'I bet you're sorry you're not in Monrosa now.'

Alice attempted to wipe her brow where water was dripping into her eyes but the bags she was carrying hit the umbrella and toppled it backwards, exposing her to the full force of the hailstones again. She gave a gasp and startled forwards, her body colliding with his. He placed a hand around her waist to steady her, drew the umbrella back up over them, and, though he knew it was wrong of him, smiled down into those grey eyes and said softly, 'I guess we're both in need of a long, hot shower.'

Her eyes widened. The hail pounded down on the umbrella. And as the light faded around them, thanks to the worsening weather, it felt as though they were the only ones on this earth.

It would be so easy to get this wrong.

He stepped back, took her bags from her. Gestured back towards the house. Gave her a smile. 'I stayed in London to make sure you're okay and here I am letting you get soaked to the bone. Come on inside; you need to get warm.'

A little while later, both of them having showered and changed, he carried two hot drinks up to the sitting room on the second floor. He expected to find Alice sitting on the sofa watching the Christmas movie he had earlier put on for them to watch, but instead she was kneeling before the Christmas tree, placing parcels under it. He knew he should let her know that he was there but there was something heart-warming about the way she rattled some of the presents as though trying to guess what was inside, the way her hands would then smooth over the paper, the way she would place the present against her chest as though invoking a well-meaning spell over it before gently placing it on the floor.

His chest tightened, realising that there would have been a time when she had liked Christmas.

He cleared his throat.

She jumped, almost toppling over the tree in the process. Standing, she studied him. She had changed into dark denim jeans and a plum-coloured wide-necked top that had fallen off one of her shoulders to reveal a cream vest-top beneath. Her hair was still wet and she had sleeked it back off her face, making her eyes, her cheekbones, her mouth seem even more pronounced than usual.

She was beautiful.

Not in a conventional way.

You could easily not spot her in a crowd. Which would be a tragedy. It was only when she spoke, when she challenged you, when you saw first-hand the essence of her spirit that you realised just how gorgeous she was.

He lowered the tray of drinks onto the coffee table beside the sofa.

He looked down at the large pile of presents under the tree and then back to her.

She shrugged. Looked uncertain for a moment, but then answered his unspoken question. 'My mum packed a whole load of presents for me, so I decided to buy you some too.'

Before he had an opportunity to respond she whipped around and, lifting a small handmade card close to the top of the tree, continued, 'You do know that soldier is spelt with a D and not a G.' She gave him a wicked grin. 'I thought I should point that out in case you ever have a need to write to the Monrosian Army.'

He held out his hand and she handed him the card. He laughed when he read his poorly formed and spelt message to Papá Noel. 'I remember writing this card! I must have been five or six and I wanted a ZX Marine commander toy soldier. My mother used to insist on us writing a card every year which was then hung from the tree for Papá Noel to read on Christmas Eve. Before my father inherited the throne from my grandfather we used to spend Christmas in different countries. My mother loved to travel. And she loved Christmas even more. She used to say that she wanted to experience Christmas in as many countries as possible.'

He stopped and studied the card again, a solid lump in his throat to see his name sprawled messily across the bottom. Christmas had used to be such a magical time in his family.

'I'm sorry… Oh, I feel terrible now, moaning about Christmas, when it must mean so much to you.'

Taken aback by the upset in her voice, he touched her arm. 'It's okay…and totally understandable why you feel the way you do about Christmas.'

She shook her head. 'No, it's not okay—you shouldn't have to listen to me cribbing about it. I could have ruined your Christmas by being all Miss Negativity.'

'I don't expect you to change how you feel about Christmas just for me…' pausing to study the parcels beneath the tree—there were at least eight bearing the logo of a landmark London department store with a similar amount of variously wrapped parcels—he asked, 'Are we ex-

pecting some guests tomorrow?' Why did that
thought bother him so much? Usually he loved
having as many people as possible surrounding him. But tomorrow…he wanted it just to
be him and Alice.

'No, they're all for us.' Reaching down, she
plucked up one of the colourfully wrapped
presents. 'My mum insisted I bring all of my
presents with me. So I decided I'd buy you an
equal amount. Now we have the same number
to open tomorrow. It only seemed fair that way.'
She gave him an uncertain smile. 'I wasn't sure
if you would have any other presents to open.'

His family were lousy present-givers. In fact,
they had stopped giving each other presents
over a decade ago. The same year that Edwin
and he had had a fierce argument with their father over Christmas dinner about a proposed
mass-tourism development on the coastline.
That had been the last time they had spent
Christmas together.

Picking up one of the presents, he touched
his finger against the red velvet bow, knocked
sideways by her thoughtfulness.

He knew she didn't like Christmas. But she
had gone out and bought presents for him.
He couldn't remember the last time someone

had done something so meaningful for him. 'Thank you.'

She blinked at his whisper. Something soft and vulnerable entered her expression.

Long seconds passed. Seconds where an initial tenderness between them drifted into an electric longing so visceral you could almost touch it. He eased her into a hug. Her body slotted against his, her arms winding around his waist. He kissed the top of her head, inhaling her light floral scent, the longing inside of him melding with a rawness, a care, a need to protect her that surged like a powerful force within him.

When they broke away, they held each other's gaze, the connection between them wild and turbulent. Alice was the first to move away. 'I should get back to my writing…' Turning as a fresh hailstorm pinged against the windows, she sighed. 'This weather is so miserable it's hard to believe that it's Christmas. Christmas is supposed to be about cold, dry days with a smattering of frost or even snow if we're lucky. Not an entire monsoon season in one week. The forecast is even worse for tomorrow. We won't even be able to get out for a walk.'

Alice was right. Christmas should have been about snow. And it should also have been about leaving the world behind. Every worry, every obligation should have been forgotten on Christmas Day. He smiled, knowing what it was he wanted to do. He was going to make this Christmas magical for her. 'My family have a ski chalet in Switzerland—let's go there.'

She made a disbelieving snort and laughed before realising that he hadn't been joking. 'I can't; I have my writing...'

'You need a break.'

He pulled out his phone from his pocket. Searched for the palace's travel office while Alice recited a long list of reasons why she couldn't go. And, when he spoke to the on-duty travel officer in Spanish, she eyed him warily as though she was trying to decipher every single word of their conversation. Details arranged, he hung up. 'The palace's jet is free. It can collect us from City Airport in three hours' time and fly us to Sion.' Checking his watch, he added, 'By nine tonight we can be in Verbier. And tomorrow we can spend the day skiing. The decision is yours whether we go or not.'

Her mouth opened. She went to speak. Stopped. 'I shouldn't...and I can't ski.'

'I can teach you. In fact, I can teach you to snowboard, which I prefer.'

'You go... I'll stay here.'

'You're not spending Christmas alone.'

'Why not? I'll be perfectly happy.'

He folded his arms. 'Will you, though?'

She reddened, gave an irked shake of her head. 'You are impossible, do you know that?' Then, throwing her arms up in the air, she shook her head, sighed and said, 'I'll go and pack.' She was almost to the door when she came to a stop and added, 'Tell the travel office to book a ticket back to London for me on the twenty-sixth. You can travel directly to Monrosa by yourself.'

Her eyes tightly shut, Alice hummed to herself. She was not afraid. The helicopter pilot knew what he was doing. Landing at night in icy conditions was a piece of cake to him. Wasn't it?

The helicopter banked. Her stomach flipped over. A tiny murmur escaped her lips. She opened her eyes to find Luis, who was seated next to her, grinning. She slapped his arm. 'It's not funny.'

He attempted a contrite smile. But then, abandoning his pretence that her horror at flying by helicopter from the airport to Verbier in the dark, through mountainous terrain, wasn't amusing, he decided instead to distract her by pointing out the town and its picturesque landmarks beneath them.

When the helicopter eventually landed on a helipad to the side of the chalet, located on a hill overlooking Verbier, she greeted terra firma with shaky legs and a heavy sigh of relief to be still alive.

A path from the landing pad to the chalet had been cleared of snow. She and Luis immediately followed it to the welcoming warmth of the chalet, while awaiting staff took care of their luggage.

Inside, Luis led her from the entranceway through various reception rooms, giving her a guided tour of the huge chalet, which even had an indoor swimming pool and cinema room.

When they finally made it to her bedroom, her luggage had already been unpacked.

Soon after, all of the chalet staff said their goodbyes, Luis reassuring them that there was no need for them to change their existing Christmas plans and that he and she would be perfectly capable of taking care of themselves for the next two days. As the lights from the staff cars made their way down the mountain she gestured around her, to the vast reception room that was softly lit with table lamps, to the huge log fire burning in the grate, filling the room with pine-scented warmth, the reflection of the flames dancing on the endless windows overlooking Verbier, and the longest and most luxurious sofa she had ever seen, and said, 'When you said a chalet, I was expecting a tiny log cabin.'

Luis grinned. 'We do own a small cabin further up in the mountains. We use it whilst skiing for refreshment breaks. We can decamp there if you'd prefer for us to be somewhere a little more intimate.'

For crazy seconds her heart folded over at the playful sparkle in his eye. But then she gave an exaggerated eye roll to compensate for her foolishness. None of this was serious to Luis. Now she could see that. He was looking for a distraction, an adventure, a new buzz. The man was an adrenaline freak. And she would be incredibly naive to believe that his attention was anything other than yet another entertaining diversion for him.

Walking over to the window, the bright lights of an outdoor Christmas tree in a far-off neighbouring property caught her attention. Spinning around, she scanned the room curiously. 'Something has been niggling away at me since we arrived and now I know what it is.' Pausing to gesture around the room, she added, 'There are no Christmas decorations.'

Leaning against the long wooden beam that

served as the mantelpiece, Luis shrugged. 'I told the staff to take them down.'

For long seconds the crackling of the fire was the only sound in the room. She tried to respond but could find no words. Tears prickled against the backs of her eyes. She never cried. She so wished he wouldn't keep ambushing her emotions by being so considerate.

She breathed in and forced out a pretty shaky laugh. 'If we're going to spend Christmas in an Alpine chalet, in one of the most picturesque winter scenes in the entire world, we are going to have to do it justice. Where are the decorations stored?'

Walking towards her, he regarded her with such a depth of concern that those damn tears threatened again. 'We can pretend tomorrow is just a normal day.'

She folded her arms. 'Work with me here, Luis. I've given up two days of writing for this. I'm going to try to embrace Christmas—okay, I'll admit I'll never be a huge fan of its madness, but for you I'll try.'

'For me?'

Her heart closed over at the quiet delight in his voice. 'Yes, for you.'

'Why?'

Because you're the kindest, most generous

person I have ever met. Because I'm tired of being sensible. I want to forget that I should be questioning everything that you do and I want to try to believe that there are good guys out there. I'm tired of fighting myself. I'm tired of pretending that I'm perfectly content in my life. I want some fun. For once in my life I just want to go with the flow and not be terrified by what-ifs.

'Because I spent three hours this morning buying gifts and I want to be able to leave them under a Christmas tree tonight.' Walking to the door that led out to the double-height hallway that held a masterpiece of design—the most incredible cantilevered wooden staircase she had ever seen—she asked, 'Now, are you going to show me where the decorations are or do I have to find them myself?'

An hour later Alice teetered on a stepladder, stretched just a little bit more, and with a grin managed to place the star on top of the enormous fir Christmas tree Luis had dragged in from outside.

It was a struggle to climb back down the ladder, thanks to Luis's hand being perilously close to her bottom as he guided her down.

When she reached the floor they both stood

back and studied the exquisite white baubles and flashing icicle lights, then turned to each other at the exact same time and high-fived one another, laughing at their mutual delight at a job well done.

But then Luis frowned at the tree. 'It's tradition in Monrosa that, when people finish decorating the tree, they kiss. It's supposed to bring good luck.'

Alice laughed. 'No, it's not.'

His eyes twinkled. 'We could make it a tradition between us.'

How nice that would be. How nice it would be to spend future Christmases with him. To know that he understood why she struggled with past Christmas memories, to know that maybe she could heal those memories with his support.

She drew in a sharp breath. And came back to reality. 'I'll be in Ireland next year and, if Kara and Edwin have their way, you'll be in Monrosa singing Christmas carols with them. There won't be any future Christmases between us.' Pausing, she met his eye. 'Will there?'

He went to answer her question but stopped. Uncertainty clouded his expression. She turned away and adjusted one of the strings of lights.

When Luis came and stood beside her she

glanced at him. Mischief was once again sparking in his eyes. He bent his head and whispered as though they were in a crowded room and didn't want anyone else to hear, 'All the more reason for us to enjoy this Christmas. Now can I kiss you or are you going to insist on debating the issue?'

She knew she should walk away, but when he was this close, when her head spun from his warm, intimate scent, from the sheer size of his body that made her feel tiny in comparison, when his gaze made her heart thump in her chest, a delicious warmth creep through her veins, she didn't want to know about logic or doing the sensible thing. 'Keep it brief.'

He laughed and hit a button on his watch. 'Is ten seconds brief enough for you?'

'That's too—' The rest of her words disappeared as his mouth found hers. It was a soft kiss, explorative and gentle. Her world shrank to the glorious heat of his mouth.

His alarm sounded.

She moved closer to him.

His arms wound around her as the alarm was silenced. His hand touched against her back where her jumper and jeans had parted. She sighed as his thumb pressed against her spine.

His alarm sounded again.

But, instead of breaking away, he silenced it again and deepened their kiss. Her chest was pressed against his, her body growing second by second more and more aware of every hard muscle of his powerful body. His kiss, his warmth, his assured movements didn't frighten her, didn't cause alarm as her previous dates had done.

On the third sounding of his alarm he pulled away from the kiss, leaving her a reeling mess of hormones and emotions.

Was she really trusting a man? After so many years of rightly protecting herself?

In the aftermath of his violence her dad had used to cry and plead for her mum's forgiveness, hugging and soothing her as though she were the most fragile thing on earth, placing tender kisses on her forehead. It had made Alice's skin crawl...yet she had also wanted to believe him.

Luis's hand cupped her cheek. 'You're so beautiful.'

She searched his eyes, looking for even a glimmer of deceit. But all she could find was honest certainty and integrity shining from his eyes. And she lost another piece of her heart to him.

CHAPTER SEVEN

'IT'S MY MUM!' Stumbling into the kitchen, yanking down a turquoise pyjama top covered in polar bears over matching shorts, Alice waved her mobile phone in the air. 'I slept in. Why didn't you wake me? I promised my mum I'd call her at nine on the dot. She's probably freaking out now, imagining all sorts of bad things happening to me.' Frantically looking about her, she mumbled, 'Not in here…the sitting room, in front of the tree.' She bolted towards the door, disappeared, but a few seconds later she was back. 'My mum thinks that I'm still in London—don't do anything to let her know otherwise.' She moved away again but darted back once more. 'And she doesn't know that I'm with you.'

Finishing off preparing their breakfast, Luis grinned. Alice's coltish legs were long and shapely. What would it be like to trail kisses along their length, to have them entwined with his? He groaned and plucked a blueberry off the top of the granola he had prepared for them, crunching down on it.

He poured himself a coffee. Not knowing where any of this was going. He knew he had to be honourable and protect her. But a hunger, a need to know her better, in every sense of that word, was tearing apart every good intention he had. To start with, he needed to stop kissing her. *Dio!* But it was addictive. The chemistry, the passion, the rightness between them was unbelievable. When he touched her he felt truly alert to the beauty and glory of life.

He strolled out to the sitting room. Alice, seated on the floor in front of the Christmas tree, was screen-chatting on her phone, which was propped up on a coffee table. She eyed him warily for a moment as he sat on the sofa opposite her, frowning when he grinned. He was going to enjoy this.

'What's the weather like?' asked a female voice.

She glanced out of the window, her eyes growing wide as she took in the heavy snow falling. He really should have checked the weather forecast before he promised her a day's skiing.

'Oh, the usual… So how are you all doing? I hope you're enjoying yourselves.'

A chorus of voices called out, 'Yes,' and then a male voice added, 'No.'

A vexed female voice immediately responded, 'Maurice, you heard what Dr Lynch said with your very own ears. Anyway, Alice doesn't want to be hearing about your new diet. Come on, Alice, give us a tour of the house.'

Alice blanched. 'Aunt Nina, there's not a lot to see.'

'Are you joking? It's the London residence of the Monrosian royal family. Of course there's things to see.'

She gave Luis a brief look, reddening. 'No.'

'Ah, Alice, you're no fun.'

Alice sighed. But then, sweeping her presents before her, she gave a wide smile, no doubt glad to find a way to move this conversation on. Lifting one up, she pulled away the wrapping paper. 'An exfoliate—thanks, Rose.'

A satisfied voice answered, 'The girl in the shop said we should all be using it, on our thighs especially, for cellulite.'

For a moment Alice looked down at her thighs in alarm.

Luis smothered a laugh. Alice glared at him.

One by one, Alice opened her presents, her

enthusiasm and warmth towards those on the other side of the screen giving no hint of her dislike of Christmas. Did she keep it secret from them?

When it came to the last present, Alice read the gift tag and said, 'Oh, Sarah, I didn't realise that you had bought me a present.'

An excited teenage voice answered back, 'I saw it when I was out shopping. I thought you'd like it.'

Opening the present, Alice frowned. And then she reddened. Turning the present towards the camera, she attempted nonchalance. 'A calendar of Edwin's brother, Prince Luis. I didn't know you were fan, Sarah?'

'I saw you in the garden—'

Leaping for the phone, Alice interrupted her. 'Thanks again, Sarah. It was lovely speaking to you all, but I'd better go. I have to get back to work.'

A voice answered, 'Of course, Ally. But hold on for a moment, I'll go somewhere where we can chat properly.'

Alice smiled fondly at the person talking, everything about her softening with affection. 'You're busy, Mum. We can talk tomorrow.'

A door closed at the other end of the line.

'That's better. This house is crazier than usual. How are you? I miss you.'

'I miss you too.'

'Are you eating okay? Are you sure you're not lonely? It seems wrong that you're all alone, especially at Christmas when you love it so much. It's not the same here without you.'

'I'm fine, Mum, honestly.' Pausing, she glanced at Luis. 'And I'm not lonely.'

'Good. I like your pyjamas.'

Alice ran a hand down over her top, shaking her head. 'I'm thirty next year, Mum. I think it's time you stopped buying me Christmas pyjamas.'

'It's too cold at this time of year to be wearing nothing in bed.'

Blushing furiously, she swung away from Luis's line of sight. 'Mum! Honestly.'

Her mother laughed and then asked, 'Will you come home at least for New Year's Eve?'

'Mum, you know that I can't. I need peace and quiet to get my writing done. You know how noisy my upstairs neighbours are.'

Her mum sighed. 'I know. I love you, Ally.'

Turning back in Luis's direction, Alice smiled into her phone. 'And I love you too. I'll be home soon. Take care and enjoy the rest of the day.'

Something hard and obstinate stuck in his throat as Alice hung up, both women giggling as they made noisy kisses to one another. He missed that simple, uncompromising love. He missed his mother.

Coming to sit opposite him, she sighed.

'Your mum doesn't know how you really feel about Christmas?' he asked.

She curled her legs underneath herself. 'There's no point in her knowing.'

'But you seem so close...'

She shrugged. 'We are, but she went through enough with my dad without having to bear the burden of how it impacted on me. For a while I was angry with her. After she left my dad I just shut down. I was angry with her for taking so long to leave him, but I was also unfairly angry with her for not staying.' Sinking further into the corner of the sofa, she added, 'I hated my dad, but I loved him too. I couldn't understand how I could feel that way. When he played professional rugby, I'd beg him not to go to work. Most months he ended up with some type of injury. Concussion, pulled muscles. When he did finally retire, he didn't do so out of choice. He hated not playing, being part of the team. That was when his drinking worsened. He'd promise that he'd stop drinking, say he was sorry. I used to believe him. My mum rarely spoke to me about what was going on; I guess she was trying to protect me. I tried to speak to her about it, but she'd tell me not to worry. So in that vacuum of silence, not sure of what was the right thing to say, I'd tell her that Dad promised that things would get better. Why did I believe him? And what if I hadn't said those things to my mum? Maybe she would have left him much sooner than she did?'

He moved over and sat beside her. 'Your father, and only he, was responsible for what happened. No one else.'

She shrugged. 'I guess you're right.'

'And will you start actually believing that? That you weren't in any way to blame for what happened?'

She didn't answer him.

'You were *not* to blame.'

She nodded, her eyes full of emotion. 'You have an incredible instinct for understanding people; you do realise that, don't you?'

He lifted up the calendar from the floor. 'Like the instinct that tells me that you're going to throw this into the bin at the earliest opportunity?'

She groaned, covering her face with her hands. 'I had forgotten about that. Sarah must have seen us together in the garden.'

'Isn't she the cousin you had the bet with?'

'Bet? No… Why…? Oh, *the bet to kiss you*. No! Sarah is only fourteen—I wouldn't be encouraging a teenager to gamble.' Taking the calendar from him, she flicked through it, laughing when he expressed his disbelief that there was a market for such a thing. 'I'm sure it'll be snapped up when I donate it to my local charity shop.'

He shook his head. 'Well, at least it'll be going to a good cause.'

She studied him. 'Are you involved in many charities as part of your royal duties?'

'I'm a patron of the national acquired brain injury charity and an ambassador for Kara's Young Adults Together, but my professional career meant that I haven't been able to dedicate myself as much as I would have liked to either of them.'

'I bet you're great in those roles though… with your energy and how engaging you are with people. And now that you're leaving powerboating you'll have more time to devote to them.'

How could he explain to her what a fraud he felt whenever advocating for any charity, when trying to influence change? As his father had liked to point out, he had achieved nothing in life other than to learn how to drive a boat really fast. 'I'm not sure I'm the best of role models. Especially as the British press has decided to label me The Reckless Prince.'

'Okay, so you're known for pushing boundaries, taking risks. But young people would relate to that. Your intuition and natural instinct to help are too valuable for you not to put them to good use.'

'I'm the last person on this earth who should be advising anyone on how to live their life, given my past. Expelled from school, a dropout from university, and for the first few years of my career I came bottom in the rankings, thanks to too many rash decisions out on the course.'

'People, especially teenagers, aren't looking for perfection. Just someone who's honest and knows what it's like to struggle at times.'

Taken aback by the passion in her voice, in her belief in him, not ready to deal with just how disorientated he felt by it, he opted to tease her instead of carrying on this conversation. 'Are you saying that I'm not perfect?'

Leaning forward, her eyes silver pools of laughter but also affection, she studied him for a few moments and answered, 'I'm starting to realise that perfect is boring.'

* * *

Luis held her gaze, not blinking, leaning closer into her. And there it was again, that magic that kept springing between them, a magic of connection and desire, a recognition, she didn't fully understand. He gave her a lopsided grin.

For a heart-soaring moment she thought he was about to kiss her but instead he took hold of the calendar Sarah had gifted her and studied the photos. 'Given that you don't rate perfection so highly, perhaps I should stage some photos of me looking a little more dishevelled—it might encourage you to keep my calendar next year.'

For June, the calendar-makers had chosen a picture of him emerging from the sea, all golden-skinned and defined muscle. The room suddenly feeling way too hot, she took hold of the calendar and placed it behind her. 'It's your turn to open your presents.'

He raised an eyebrow, his eyes shining with amusement. Shaking his head, he stood and gathered up all of his presents. 'I'm hungry. I'll open them over breakfast.'

She stood too and gestured towards her pyjamas. 'I'll go and get changed first.'

His eyes twinkled. 'Don't. They're cute. And

it's nice to see you wearing something colourful for a change.'

'You sound like my mother. She's always telling me that I should wear more colourful clothes, these pyjamas being a case in point. She insists on buying me a set every year. If I hadn't worn them for our call, I'd never have heard the end of it.'

'What's with your obsession with dark-coloured clothes anyway?'

She shrugged. It was just habit.

Because they make me feel safe. I don't want to stand out, be a target for anyone.

She blinked at that realisation. 'It saves time in the morning, and anyway I hate shopping. Sticking mostly to black and navy cuts out any time-wasting.'

Not looking convinced by her reasoning, he contemplated her pyjama top. 'Turquoise suits you...red would look great on you too.'

She rolled her eyes. 'What, are you a fashion consultant now? And I thought you said you were hungry.'

'So I did.' He said it in such a low rumble, mischief glittering in his eyes, that she bolted for the door and in the kitchen went straight for the safety of sitting at the dining table, glad to be able to hide her legs from how Luis kept staring at them. God, she hoped she didn't have cellulite. A tummy given to bloating was enough to contend with.

The dining table was set into an alcove made entirely of glass, and cantilevered over the mountain. Heavy snow continued to fall on the sloping glass roof of the alcove, the village below invisible in the snowstorm. 'It's like being inside a snow globe,' she said.

'Except this has underfloor heating,' Luis said with a chuckle, bringing freshly brewed tea and coffee to the table.

While she tucked into the rich, flaky layers of a croissant, Luis ate a bowl of granola and yoghurt, and described the hair-raising off-piste ski runs he had done in isolated spots, having been dropped in by helicopter, shrugging off her disbelief that he had continued to take such risks even after once being caught up in an avalanche.

When they had both finished eating, he lifted up the largest of his presents, testing its weight in the palm of his hand. Thrown by how keenly he was studying the present, the expectation in his expression, she cringed and said, 'They're only small tokens…nothing special…don't expect too much.'

Unwrapping the first present, he studied it. 'A bonsai tree. Why a bonsai tree?'

She laughed. 'It's a reminder that great things of beauty take time and attention and patience. I hope you'll look at it and remember that it's good to slow down and that life doesn't have to be lived at a hundred miles an hour.'

He eyed her suspiciously. 'Why do I get the feeling there's going to be a theme here?'

Next came the aromatherapy pressure-point kit, which he received with a wry smile, and then the dark green polo shirt she had bought him, loving both the softness of the fabric and how it was a perfect match for the flecks of green in his eyes.

Opening the handcrafted dark praline chocolates, he asked in surprise, 'My favourite flavour—how did you know?'

'Just a lucky guess.'

And the fact that you ate that lone chocolate at the bottom of my sweet tin with such relish the other night.

Next came the limited-edition landscape print of the Thames at night. Her final present to him was a book. He held the hardback, studying the portrait painting on the cover before asking, 'You're not going to throw this one at me, are you?'

Alice laughed. 'Unless you provoke me.' Pausing, she wondered at the sense in giving it to him. Would he be interested? She swallowed. Suddenly wanting him to care, to want to know more about her. 'It's a biography on Lady Maud Radford—my PhD subject.'

'Why did you choose Lady Radford?'

'In the late nineteenth century she owned a huge estate close to where my mum now lives. When she was alive she divided her time between the estate and her house in London. She was very influential in Anglo-Irish politics but what she achieved hasn't been recognised because of her more famous son, the poet Henry Radford. She was incredibly progressive in her advocacy for women's rights and the rights of all children to a free education. Her views influenced education reforms and I think her contribution to that deserves to be acknowledged.'

Opening the book, he studied the photographs of Lady Radford and her family in the centre pages and then, reaching to touch the delicate branches of the bonsai tree, he said, 'I can see why it took you three hours to select all of these gifts; thank you for choosing them so carefully.'

Taken aback by the emotion in his voice, she

responded, 'I'm sure these are nothing in comparison to the gifts that you usually receive.'

He shook his head. 'I receive gifts in an official capacity, but I always donate those to charity, or they are placed in the royal archive—and as for more personal gifts...well, as a family we haven't exchanged gifts in years.'

She pushed her plate aside, wanting to reach out to him, to ease the troubled lines now pinching at the corners of his eyes. 'I'll have to make sure to send you a present every Christmas.'

Her heart turned over to see him smile. But then he gave her an apologetic look. 'I thought, given your feelings on Christmas, that you wouldn't want a gift.'

She waved away his disquiet. 'Oh, I didn't want anything.' She gestured to the snow outside. 'To experience a proper white Christmas is more than enough.'

Liar! Okay, you hadn't actually thought about it up to now, but now that he has brought it up you do want something. Nothing big. Just a token to know he thought about it. Something to remember these days.

'I'll have to make it up to you next year.'

She gave him an uncertain shrug, her heart sinking, knowing there would be no reason for him to give her a gift next year. How would she

feel about Christmas next year? Would she re-
live time and time again the whirlwind, the unexpected turns of this Christmas? How would
she feel knowing that these few intoxicating
days would never happen again?

For a crazy moment, as silence feel between
them and he held her gaze, she thought they
were sharing the same identical thoughts. But
then he stood and, walking away, said, 'Come
with me.' He led her back to the sitting room,
where he opened a drawer in a console table.
From it he took out a parcel wrapped in gold
paper and handed it to her.

Her heart singing with pleasure and anticipation, she opened the present. Seeing what
was inside, she laughed. 'Wow, my very own
Our Place—or should I say *Our lace?*—soccer
jersey.'

His eyes danced with merriment. 'We can become their first official fans.' Then he pointed
towards the branches of the Christmas tree. 'Do
you spot anything different to what we hung
last night?'

Puzzled, she glanced over the branches of
the tree, until she saw a small white bag with
the world-famous gold insignia of Jarrad Jewellers of Bond Street sitting close to one of the
flashing icicle lights.

She pointed at it, not sure where this was going.

Lifting the bag from the tree, he handed it to her.

'It's for me?'

'Well, I don't think it will suit me,' he answered.

Inside the bag there was a white velvet box. Opening it, she gasped before lifting out the falling cluster of white-gold flowers inset with diamonds on a white-gold chain.

'This can't be for me.'

Taking it from her, he placed it around her neck. She shivered as his hands touched her skin. 'My prize fund for winning the World Series was substantial. It's nice to be able to share it with someone.'

She closed her eyes. How could she refuse to accept his gift, given those words, given the emotional punch they delivered right into the centre of her heart? Meeting his gaze, she felt realisation barrel through her—he might have a hectic social life and a wide network of friends but perhaps he too understood what it was to feel alone.

She touched her lips against his cheek. 'Thank you.' And then stepped away, terrified by just how emotional she was feeling. She tucked the necklace beneath her pyjama top, confused by what it signified. Did he give such generous gifts to everyone in his life?

Returning to the kitchen, they both began to clear away the dishes. Wanting to lighten the mood between them, she said, 'Yesterday when I was shopping a store assistant asked me if she could help me. I must have looked *really* lost for her to have taken the time out from the chaos around her. Anyway, she asked who I was buying for and I was so frazzled I blurted out that it was for a prince. Without even blinking, she immediately directed me towards the pet section; she thought I was referring to my dog!'

Moving his gifts to a side table, he laughed. 'Are you saying I might have received some dog biscuits as a present?'

Searching for the glass cupboard, in order to stack away some unused juice glasses, she said, 'Well, I was pretty desperate…and they had the most adorable dog beds in the shape of Santa's sleigh. But there was no way you'd have fitted into them.'

She grinned at Luis's laughter and, moving to the sink to rinse their plates and cups, she admitted, 'I wanted a dog so badly when I was a child, but my dad wouldn't let me. He said they were more trouble than they were worth.'

Coming alongside her, he shook his head in disbelief. 'Not worth the loyalty and affection and endless games of chase? Really?'

She snorted, something freeing in her, at his outrage. She had never thought she'd see the day when she would be able to laugh over anything concerning her dad.

Rinsing done, she watched as Luis settled himself against the counter opposite her. 'We had four dogs. Our mother allowed us to adopt one each on our tenth birthday provided we proved responsible enough by taking care of the family dog, Snuggles.'

This time she gave a hoot of laughter. 'Snuggles! What a great name.'

He regarded her with such warmth and affection that her heart felt as light and free as the snowflakes floating past the window. 'Yeah, it's a cool name, but not for him unfortunately—he was a grumpy schnauzer who refused to be cuddled.'

She laughed but in truth she was seriously distracted, thanks to how good he looked propped like that against the worktop. Blue shirt over blue jeans and tan boots. Height and power. Narrow waist, long and muscular legs. Hair a few centimetres longer than at the wedding. She preferred this length. Clean-shaven—

this she also preferred, liking the warmth, the buzz of his skin against hers. He tilted his head in question. He was waiting for her to say something.

What had they been talking about? Dogs. Of course!

Now she just needed to find something to say. 'So…yes…what…what was the name of the dog you adopted?'

Moving away to grab his phone from the dining table, he came and stood beside her. 'He was a cross-breed from the local dog shelter.' Opening up his photo gallery, he scrolled through endless photos.

She caught brief glimpses of beautiful buildings and beaches and powerboats and gorgeous women. Okay, so these women were often in mixed groups, with nothing to suggest that they were more than just friends to Luis. But they were there. They were all part of his life, a life she knew nothing about. Luis had a whole life and friends and relationships she knew nothing about. That thought was odd…and disconcerting.

Finally pausing at a picture, he showed it to her. Her heart melted. 'Oh, gosh! He's so adorable.' The grinning dog looked like a mixture between a Wheaten and a Scottish terrier.

'Yes, he was…his name was Rocky,' he said, his voice full of emotion. 'I hated boarding school, not just because of the stupid need to conform and to obey rules that only made sense a hundred years ago but… I was homesick, for Rocky especially. After I was expelled my father was intent on sending me to a school in America but thankfully my aunt, Princess Maria, and her husband, Johan, persuaded him to allow me to stay with them. And, best of all, Rocky and I were reunited—my aunt smuggled him out of the palace without my father knowing. He was furious when he found out and accused my aunt of spoiling me—he thought I shouldn't be allowed to have Rocky as a form of punishment.'

'Were you happy living with your aunt and uncle?' she asked, hoping that he had been— what must it have been like to lose his mother and then be sent away to another country?

'Yes…in some ways. I had Rocky, and my aunt and uncle indulged me in whatever sport I was obsessed with at any particular time— I rode, sailed, played soccer and cricket, took up abseiling and kite surfing, and then I discovered a passion for motocross. I know they had concerns for my safety and the appropriateness of my involvement with some of the sports, but they always came to watch me compete.' He shifted away from the worktop and, grabbing hold of some paper towel and a spray bottle, he began to wipe the kitchen table with quick, wide, arching movements. 'My father refused to speak to me for over a year. He said I'd brought shame on the family by being expelled from his alma mater.'

'Why were you expelled?'

Head bowed in concentration as he continued to clean the length of the table that could seat at least ten, he answered, 'As I already said, I never settled in. The school was constantly calling my father over my behaviour. What finally got me expelled was when I let some pigs from the neighbouring farm loose in the school.'

Trying not to laugh, she asked, 'And what was the purpose of that little stunt?'

Tossing the paper towel into the bin, he answered, 'I was bored, and I had a science exam an hour later I was going to fail.'

'You wanted to be expelled?'

He folded his arms. 'Yes.' For a few seconds he considered her, shuffled on his feet, looking increasingly uncomfortable. He looked away from her. 'I wanted to get home to Rocky.'

'Did you tell your dad how—?'

He interrupted her, 'We don't have that type of relationship. After my mother died, he didn't want to know about our lives or what we wanted.'

'Losing your mum must have been hard for him too.'

Something dark flashed across his expression. He refused to look at her. His jaw working, he let out an angry breath. She shrank backwards.

He swung his head back in her direction. His eyes widened. 'Alice... I'm sorry.' He unfolded his arms. 'I'm angry with my father, not you.' And then on a sigh he said, 'And you're right. Her death did destroy him...and us as a family.'

Butterflies of panic still soaring in her stomach, she breathed against them. Any sign of annoyance panicked her. Impatient customers made her clumsy. Older men especially. She knew she had to stop equating other people to her father. She had thought that she had made inroads in doing so in recent years. But just now with Luis, it was as though she was looking for any sign that he would hurt her. Which was unfair, she knew that, but deep down she was increasingly panicking at how much he was getting inside her head...and heart.

'Did you tell your brothers about how much you disliked school?'

'No. Edwin was always trying to appease my father and Ivo was never to be seen. He spent most of his time painting model soldiers in his room and then he became obsessed with rowing. He and I are alike in our passion for sport…and in our desire to get away from Monrosa.' He turned away and plucked a piece of paper from the noticeboard. 'The chef has left details on preparing tonight's dinner. I had better read it and try to decipher his instructions.'

She had never spoken to anyone before about her childhood, hating those memories. She glanced at the white velvet jewellery box, at the snow now falling in slow, dancing swirls, at her gifts to Luis, realising that sometimes, sharing what was deep inside, you could be the most valuable gift of all. 'I had no one to speak to when I was a child. I know how frightening that can be.'

He studied her before moving towards her, his eyes so gentle, so compassionate, swallowing up her heart. 'I wish you had had a Rocky in your life back then.'

She swallowed. Laughed in surprise, hot tears pressing against the backs of her eyes. 'I wish I'd had a Rocky too.'

His hand rested on her arm, his touch one of comfort. 'I reckon it's time we started having some fun. What do you think?'

She nodded. 'Agreed.' Looking out at the falling snow, she asked, 'Will we get to go skiing?'

'Unfortunately I don't think so.' Walking over to the window, he looked out. 'We'll need to think of something else we can do.' He turned around, a wicked gleam in his eye.

She braced herself.

'Do you have a swimsuit with you?' he asked.

'I'm on a skiing holiday—what do you think?'

'In that case I'll find you one.'

Following Luis as he rushed down the stairs to the basement with a little too much enthusiasm for her liking, she asked, 'Are we going swimming?'

Holding open the entrance door to the spa and pool area, he grinned. 'Something even better.'

She came to a stop. 'What?'

'It's a surprise.'

'I don't like surprises.'

'How about, just for today, you take a chance on relinquishing some of the control you insist on single-handedly gripping onto and let someone else make a few decisions on your behalf?'

She refused to budge even when he gestured for her to step into the spa area. 'What if they're decisions I don't like?'

He fake-considered this. 'Well, I agree that you mightn't like it immediately...' he paused and considered her with a dangerous and sexy glint in his eye '...but trust me: the pain and discomfort will be worth it.'

She swallowed. 'Okay, so now I'm worried.'

He lowered his head, looked directly into her eyes. 'I'll never hurt you. You do know that, don't you?'

Her heart kicked. Would she be terribly naïve to believe him? 'I'll hold you to that promise, you know.' Not waiting for a response, she stepped into the spa.

Luis followed her and opened a door to the side of the pool, the lights inside flickering on automatically to reveal shelves piled high with snow-white towels, dressing gowns and slippers. Brand-new swimming costumes still bearing their designer labels hung from a rail.

'Take your pick,' he said, walking to a row of wardrobes. He opened a door and took out a pair of pale blue swimming trunks and then grabbed hold of a towel and dressing gown.

'I'll meet you by the pool.'

Eyeing the swimsuits, she considered the only

black item on the rail but replaced it, realising just how tiny it was. It certainly wasn't designed for someone capable of eating an entire tin of chocolates in one afternoon. She stared at the other swimsuits. Why couldn't there at least be one practical item amongst them? They were all cut way too suggestively. She eventually plucked the least revealing costume in her size from the rail and, armed with a dressing gown and towel, she went to the changing rooms.

The swimming-pool changing areas she had ever frequented had featured the triple delights of musty odours, damp floors and temperamental showers. Here, the changing area consisted of six individual changing rooms, all the size of a small apartment, complete with a tropical shower, every beauty and hair product you could wish for, a TV and sofa and way too many mirrors. Stripping, she pulled on her swimming costume and after a quick grimace at her reflection she put on her dressing gown, yanking the belt tight.

Once she was out at the pool, her heart did several kicks when she spotted Luis waiting for her dressed in only his blue trunks. She sighed. His body was even hotter than she had thought it would be. His abs were like a tightly sprung mattress.

She gestured to the pool. 'You go ahead. I'll follow you in a few minutes,' she said, and darted to sit on a lounger, needing to gather herself.

But he had other ideas. 'We're not going swimming.'

She stared in confusion at the flip-flops he held out to her before reluctantly taking them. Pulling on his dressing gown and stepping into his own pair of flip-flops, he opened the door that led out to a covered terrace and the heavy blanket of snow beyond.

'We're going out…in that?' she asked, her voice as shrill as a bag of cats.

'We sure are.'

'We'll freeze.'

He gave her a stern look. 'Are you already refusing to give up control?'

Stepping into her flip-flops, she shook her head. 'I've always said you're dangerous, and you're doing nothing to dispel that impression.'

He chuckled. 'You haven't seen anything yet.'

Outside she squealed in shock at the wall of cold that slammed into her. Out on the sloping gardens the snow had drifted into high banks. He took her hand. 'Number one rule: don't stand still.'

He led her off the terrace and along a covered path that ran alongside the chalet. At the end of the path he opened the door to his right.

Stepping in, she breathed in the warm pine-scented air, shivering in relief. 'A sauna!'

He nodded, removed his flip-flops and dressing gown and went and sat high up on a bench, settling himself into the corner, a happy grin on his face.

He watched her. Daring her to give up control of the situation.

She'd show him.

Pulling off her gown, she went and sat in the opposite corner. 'Well, this is nice.'

He laughed but didn't say anything.

He closed his eyes. She did too. But then she peeled one open. Was he as chilled-out as he seemed? There was a faint silver star just below his right knee, a fresh bruise on his collarbone. Did he work out in the gym? Was that what gave him that impossibly flat stomach and biceps that could crush you? Her heart did a quickstep as she took in the long length of his eyelashes. He would have been too beautiful but for the unbalance in the shape of his lips—his bottom lip was slightly fuller. And she found it ever so cute…and sexy. She could spend a whole morning nibbling it. She shut her

eyes, imaging waking up next to him…prefer-
ably naked and to his caresses. She shuffled
in her seat, a tingling sensation in her limbs as
she imagined his mouth and hands exploring
her body. Heat spread along her limbs. What
would it be like to have him between her legs?
An ache unfurled low in her belly. She had
never held a man… How would it feel? Would
she know what to do?

'Ready for some fun?'

She leapt at Luis's quietly spoken question.

'A cold shower perhaps,' she suggested.

He stood with a chuckle. 'Something much
better.' At the door of the sauna he said, 'We'll
cool off outside.'

She stared out at the heavy drift of snow beyond the path and despite the searing heat of the
sauna she shivered. 'You have to be joking me.'

'Nope.' He held out his hand.

She refused to budge. He folded his arms,
settling against the doorframe.

For more than a minute they held a silent
standoff, eyeing each other stubbornly.

With an exasperated exhale she stood up. He
clearly wasn't going to back down and the open
door was letting all of the heat out.

Passing Luis, she gave him the evil eye and
took a few tentative steps outside. She gasped

loudly and was so befuddled by the cold that she didn't fight him when he took hold of her hand and broke into a jog, pulling her with him.

Out in the open, beyond the covered walkway, the falling snow made her blink hard. They were heading directly for a huge snowdrift. She didn't want to do this. It was way too cold. She tried to pull Luis to a stop, but their momentum was too great. She screamed and fell into the icy blanket face first. She rolled onto her back. Screamed again. Screamed even more. Wanting to kill Luis. But then she heard herself laugh. Something freeing in her. It was Christmas morning and she was rolling in the Alpine snow with the most incredible man she had ever met. If this could happen to her, what endless possibilities were out there for her?

She gasped when fresh snow landed on her. Luis was pelting her with it! She gripped some herself and flung it at him. Laughing. Buzzing with happiness. He grabbed hold of her and they tumbled in the snow, their laughter rolling down the mountainside. He came to a stop lying on top of her, his twinkling eyes holding hers captive. Eyes that soon darkened, and, placing a kiss on her cheek and then on her mouth, he whispered, 'Happy Christmas.'

Her heart lurched. She wanted so much more with him.

Standing, Luis helped her up and lifted her into his arms. He carried her back to the sauna, grinning as she demanded that he let her down.

Inside the sauna he gently lowered her down and as he shut the door she laughed, shaking her entire body. 'That was so good.' Adrenaline was pounding through her. She high fived him. And then rubbed some snow from his collarbone.

They were now supposed to move back into their respective corners. But instead they just smiled goofily at one another. And then his eyes wandered lazily down over her body, lingering on her red swimsuit. Her skin, already on fire from the snow, took on a different heat.

'I told you that red would suit you.'

Her heart shuddered and stalled, the approval in his voice and eyes mesmerising.

His hand touched lightly against the cut-out seam above her hip. He twisted his finger into the fabric and pulled her forward, inch by slow inch. She didn't resist. Instead she smiled. Wanting this oh, so badly.

His mouth came to her ear. 'You're incredibly special.'

Her knees weakened.

His mouth moved down to nuzzle against her neck.

Her knees gave up and buckled, her body collapsing against his. His mouth found hers. They both groaned into the kiss. His hands moved to her back. Stroking, caressing her bare skin. His mouth took control of hers. Hot, probing, sensual. Leading the kiss. Pushing her to places she had never been before.

Dizzying desire flooded her, a solid ache beginning to throb in her core. His hands moved to run over her body, as though he wanted to know intimately every inch of her. Her hips, her bottom, her belly. Her body was moulded to his. The ache in her widened. Without conscious thought her body began to move against his, searching, hunting for a place that would ease the burning hunger inside of her.

They staggered backwards, Luis landing on the bench behind him. She stayed with him, her legs wrapping about his waist. As if this was the most normal thing in the world. Desire, hot and liquid, flowed through her.

She deepened the kiss, wanting more. His hand touched her side, running along her ribs, grazing over the side of her breast. She shuddered.

His hands moved under her swimsuit, one

thumb touching against her nipple, the other running along the sensitive skin of her bottom. She jerked into him, deepened the kiss. She cried out as his hardness pressed against her. Cried out again when his tongue flicked over the light fabric, doing little to hide the bud of her nipple.

Her head spun as he whispered words to her, words adoring her body.

She was hurtling towards an edge no man had ever brought her to.

Her body felt ripe, wanton. Emotion and passion spun together, casting a spell on her. She felt powerful and desirable. Did he realise what he was giving her? The gift to enjoy her own body.

He knew exactly what he was doing, his mouth on her breast, his fingers pressing against her. He flicked the material of her swimsuit aside, his fingers finding the most sensitive points of her body. She gasped, spinning away from the conscious world to one solely filled with pleasure and need.

His mouth sucked harder. His fingers moved faster. He knew exactly the chaos he was wreaking on her.

She gasped again. Screamed. And fell into a long pulse of pleasure, her head thrown back.

Wave after wave of ecstasy convulsed through her. She clung to him, her head thrown back, the hard press of his body driving her pleasure on and on.

When it had finally passed she collapsed against him.

He stroked her hair. Kissed her along her cheek. And whispered with a heartbreaking tenderness, 'I want to be with you.'

She nodded. But embarrassment had her bury her head even more into his shoulder. She wasn't supposed to have done that. She had totally lost control. What was she going to do? And all of a sudden she wanted to cry, feeling raw and exposed and vulnerable. How was she going to tell him?

She pulled back. Met his eye.

He grinned, pleased with himself. The desire in his eyes stole her breath away.

She breathed in deeply, searching for a way to tell him. 'I told you that I've never had a proper boyfriend.'

'Yes...so?'

He had no idea. She swallowed hard. 'I haven't had a proper relationship in every sense.'

He nodded but was still clearly puzzled, and then she saw realisation hit his eyes. 'Do you mean that you've never slept with anyone?'

She cringed at the incredulity in his voice. Standing, her limbs weak, she stepped back and whispered, 'Even what just happened there...' she felt herself go even redder '...it hasn't happened with a man before. I thought you should know before we do anything.'

Speechless, Luis stared at her, trying to gain control of his thoughts. And then he stood, fighting back the urge to pace. *Dio!* Sleeping with her was out of the question now. He needed air. He needed to clear his head. He needed to think straight before he said anything stupid. But instead he pulled her into a hug, his heart way too big for his chest, guessing as to why she had never slept with a man before.

Her body was rigid. He cursed. She must have seen just how thrown he was. He grappled for words, the physical desire he felt for her fighting against the need to protect her.

He sensed her about to pull away. He placed his hand on her hair, stroking it, wanting somehow to communicate with her that he understood even if he couldn't find the right way to express that right now. He mumbled out some words. 'I don't... I can't...'

She pushed against his chest, breaking away. Grabbing hold of her dressing gown, she pulled it on, refusing to look at him.

What was he supposed to say, to do?

She bolted out of the sauna. Cursing, he grabbed hold of his own dressing gown and chased after her. He followed her through the pool room and up the stairs to the ground floor. In the entrance hallway she turned to him, her expression devoid of all emotion. 'I need to get dressed. I'll see you later.'

'I can't be the first.'

She winced at that, but then with a shrug spun away.

Dio! He was getting this so wrong. He pulled in a long breath, trying to quell his panic. Her bare feet landed on the first wooden step of the oak staircase. And then the second. And the third. He was a quick thinker, had never been lost for words before. What was wrong with him?

She was nearing the top of the stairs. He couldn't let her go without explaining himself to her, without trying to say why he could never sleep with her. 'I have never wanted to be with someone as much as I want to be with you.'

At the top of the stairs she spun around and studied him. Her expression was sceptical. 'You must find it hard to understand why someone my age has never slept with anyone before now.

Odd even.' She paused, her mouth tightening. 'Your reaction is understandable.'

He climbed the stairs, hating how as he drew nearer she backed away into the corner of the double-storey height balcony window that gave an endless view of the neighbouring mountainside.

He flexed his fists. For the first time in as long as he could remember he was going to be truly honest with another person, and his heart was pounding at the prospect of doing so. 'I have never taken sleeping with someone lightly. I am not into one-night stands or casual hook-ups.' He paused, not quite believing he was actually admitting all of this. 'I know it might sound old-fashioned but for me making love to someone is about intimacy and respect and care for the other person.'

She shook her head as though trying to understand what she had just heard. 'So…what are you saying…that you don't feel those things for me?'

'No! No…what I'm trying to say and doing so badly is that you're leaving tomorrow… sleeping with you would be so wrong. I wanted to spend Christmas supporting you, not complicating your life even more or possibly hurting you.'

She tossed her head back. 'Who says I'll get hurt? And maybe you're not into casual flings…but what if I am? You're the one who keeps telling me to lighten up. Well, maybe for once I just want to do something reckless.'

He raised an eyebrow. His lips twitched.

She stared at him, clearly unimpressed that he might find humour in her newly found rebellion. And then she swung around and looked out of the window, but not before he saw her mouth twitch too. Then on a sigh she said, 'It's stopped snowing. Let's head out. You can give me a snowboarding lesson like you promised.'

He could understand her need to escape from this conversation that was awkward and frankly way too close to the bone in revealing the connection that was between them, but there was more he needed to say before they escaped for the slopes. He went and stood beside her. Her eyes shifted for a brief moment towards him before she resumed staring out onto the silent white landscape outside. 'You're a beautiful, smart and brilliant woman. If you weren't Kara's cousin, if my life weren't such a mess at the moment…if I didn't care for you as much as I do…if making love wasn't so damn complicated, then I would be dragging you into my bedroom and into my bed right now and

I wouldn't be releasing you until well into the New Year. But instead I want to be your friend… I want to be able to ring you in the future. I want to be able to face you at family events without any awkwardness. And most of all, I don't want to hurt you.'

'Who said you would hurt me?'

There was a fire in her eyes that reminded him of the first night they had met. Memories of her kiss, chasing after her through the palace gardens, the disappointment of seeing her drive away and the feeling that something important had escaped his grasp, had him say softly, 'Maybe I'm trying not to be hurt myself.'

Snuggled into the corner of the sofa, Alice tried to focus on her book but her gaze kept shifting over to study Luis. For their dinner earlier he had changed into grey trousers and a white shirt, leaving the top two buttons undone. Head bowed, he was reading the book she had gifted him but how much he was taking in she wasn't sure, given that he was constantly checking his phone.

Was he waiting for someone to call or message him? A woman perhaps? She closed her eyes, dread forming in the pit of her stomach.

She had spent most of the summer before she had started secondary school alone and isolated, having been dumped from her friendship group because they were going to a different school to her. One evening she had heard beeping and located its source to an unfamiliar phone she had found in her dad's jacket pocket. Confused, she had brought it into the kitchen, asking him if he had bought a new phone and why there were so many messages from one of her mum's close friends.

Her mum had cried. Her dad had yelled. And Alice had soaked up the way her dad had twisted the blame onto her, telling her that it was she who was responsible for her mum's devastation.

The lies people told. The games they played. And the self-destruct buttons they so easily pressed. And here she was, a perfect case in point. Instead of coming to her senses and counting her blessings that she hadn't slept with Luis earlier she was actually even more attracted to him than ever. Not only was she constantly reliving in her head the feel of his mouth on her breast, the magic of his fingers, the waves of bliss that had whipped through her body, but hearing him talk so sensitively about lovemaking, hearing the passion and sincerity in his voice, the way his gaze darkened when he had said that he had never desired anyone more than her, had her completely spellbound. And this afternoon, as she had watched him so effortlessly freestyle snowboard, the way he so patiently lifted her up time and time again after her disastrous attempts to stand upright, never mind actually snowboard, he had got even further under her skin.

She shifted in her seat and pressed a hand on her burning cheeks. And groaned as her glute muscles screamed in protest.

'Are you ok?' Luis asked.

She nodded but grimaced as she attempted to manoeuvre herself into a comfortable position and admitted, 'I don't think I'll be able to walk tomorrow. They might have to carry me onto the plane.'

He smiled but didn't say anything. Wood crackled in the fireplace. Tomorrow they would be saying goodbye. It was for the best. She had to get back to work, and Luis to Monrosa.

His phone pinged. She jumped at the sudden noise. He grabbed hold of the phone and smiled as he hit play on the video message he had been sent, a chorus of voices wishing him a happy Christmas from the Bahamas. But then with a sigh he put the phone back down on the velvet armrest of his chair.

'It wasn't the message you've been waiting for all evening?'

He frowned at her question but then shrugged.

It was none of her business but suddenly she really, *really* wanted to know whose message or call he was waiting for. She opened her mouth, looking for a subtle way of phrasing her question but quickly abandoned that search, the memory of her dad's phone burning in her soul.

'She must be pretty special to warrant how distracted you have been all evening.'

Closing his book and placing it on the coffee table, he sat back in his chair and studied her.

She blinked at the open way he considered her, as though he was trying to find the solution to a particularly difficult puzzle. 'If there were another woman in my life I wouldn't have kissed you the way I did this morning. I'm not that type of man.' He said it with such a softly spoken seriousness that for a moment she almost believed him, but then all her doubts and mistrust, driven by how raw and vulnerable she felt after their intimacy earlier, made her ask, 'Well, who are you waiting for, then?'

'You don't believe anything I say, do you?'

The disappointment in his voice made her wince but something deep inside her wanted to push him. She wanted to know that everything he had said to her earlier that day about why he wouldn't sleep with her was a lie. She was just a convenient distraction.

He wasn't really attracted to her. Did he think she was going to fall for all that baloney he had spun her? 'I know first-hand the signs of a man having an affair.'

'How can I be having an affair when we're not in a relationship?' he asked.

She wanted the ground to open up and swallow her swiftly. Why on earth had she so clumsily accused him of being involved with someone else? 'You know what I mean. I'd hate to think that there's a woman out there being hurt right now and that I have something to do with it. My dad had an affair and it nearly destroyed my mum.'

She waited for him to respond, a fire in her wanting to get things out in the open. With a start she realised she wanted a fight. She never wanted to fight. She hated confrontation. But here she was, deliberately antagonising him, wanting to push him further and further. Wanting to see the real man. Would he flip like her dad? Would she get to see the real man—the anger, the denials, the manipulation?

She jumped out of her seat. 'See, this is why I hate Christmas. Everything goes wrong.'

Standing up, he stabbed some numbers into his phone, his mouth a tight grimace, and handed the phone to her. 'Feel free to check through all of my messages. Maybe then you'll believe me.'

She took the phone and stared at it, the fire inside her dying, to be replaced by shame. Handing the phone back to him, she could barely meet his stare. 'I'm sorry…that was un-called for.'

He said nothing.

Embarrassment made her throat close over. She walked over to the fireplace, studied the photos there of a young Luis and his family on skiing trips, looking so incredibly happy, Luis always standing at his dad's side, more often than not pulling a goofy pose.

She closed her eyes. And said with her back still to him, 'I'm scared of being hurt.' Turning, she studied him. 'It's easier to assume the worst in people rather than to be let down.'

'That's an unfair way to approach life…not just for the other people involved but also for yourself. You're pushing away good people because of the few and you're robbing yourself of a full life.'

She wanted to look away, she wanted to walk away from the truth in his words, but, pulling in a breath, she said, 'But it will keep me safe.'

There it was again, that sad, disappointed look of his that cut her to the quick.

'People need to be believed in.'

She shrugged. 'I'm not sure it's something that I can ever do—truly believe in everything that another person says.'

He walked over to her. 'Do you believe in what you say yourself, Alice? Maybe you should start there?'

She laughed. Not understanding his point. But then she stopped and stepped away from him. Her past insistence that she was content in her life, that she wasn't lonely, ringing hollow. She picked up a photo from the mantelpiece. 'Your mum was incredibly beautiful, and you look so like your dad when he was a younger man.'

He stared at the photo. 'I hadn't seen it before but there is a resemblance... It was my father I was waiting to hear from. I told Edwin earlier that I was delaying my return to Monrosa until the thirtieth. Apparently, my father is furious that I've cancelled my return yet again.'

Flipping a switch on the wall, throwing the entire room into darkness with the exception of the light from the fire and the Christmas tree, he went to the terrace doors and, opening one, stepped outside. 'Come and see the stars.'

She stood at the doorway and shuddered. 'It's bitterly cold.'

He gave no response but instead, grabbing hold of a shovel hidden in an outside alcove, dug a path in the snow out to the terrace's balustrade. Path cleared, he turned and answered, 'Magic only happens when we take risks.'

She rolled her eyes but took a few steps out onto the terrace. She shivered fiercely but then laughed, the shock of the cold, the endless stars overhead, invigorating and magical.

She wrapped her arms around herself, dancing on the balls of her feet to stay warm. 'Why have you delayed returning to Monrosa?'

His concentration fixed on stargazing, he answered, 'Because I'm hoping to persuade you to stay here with me for a few more days and then travel to the New Year's Eve ball in Monrosa with me.'

'What? Are you kidding me?' Her voice echoed down the valley. Was he serious? She gave him a disbelieving look. He shrugged. Shrugged! After landing that bombshell on her.

'I'm going back to London tomorrow.'

'Aren't you enjoying it here?'

Thrown, she paused. 'Yes… No… That's not the point.'

'Another few days and you'll master snow-boarding.'

'Oh, please, we both know that is never going to happen—I'm way too uncoordinated.'

'If you allow yourself another few days of forgetting about your thesis, I'll guarantee that in the New Year you'll have the energy to tackle it again.' His eyes dancing, his voice dropping to a husky timbre, he added, 'And I'm more than happy to keep you distracted until then…in whatever way you'd like.'

She paused from crazily hopping from one foot to the other. Her eyes widened, her cheeks grew hot. He smiled, remembering this morning, remembering her falling apart in his arms. Sleeping together might be out of the question but that didn't mean that they couldn't find fun in other ways.

She frowned. 'Hold on. Are you claiming to be staying here entirely for my benefit?' Not waiting for him to respond, she added, 'I'm calling you out on that. My guess is that you don't want to go back to Monrosa and I'm an excuse for you not doing so.'

She was wrong. Well, sort of. He did think staying here would benefit her. The tiredness beneath her eyes was vanishing. The tension, the preoccupation, the distractedness he had seen in her in London were all fading away too. 'Perhaps it's the right decision for both of us right now.'

She let out an impatient breath that came out like a frosted cloud from her mouth. 'Will you stop twisting things and tell me straight why you want to stay here for another few days?'

That was a good question, given the conversation they'd just had—her mistrust, her prickly, guarded suspicion should have had him happily waving goodbye to her tomorrow. But he got why she was so wary of trusting him. Yes, it frustrated him, even hurt him, but there was so much more to Alice than the cynical wariness she had developed no doubt thanks to her father's behaviour. He enjoyed her company, her intelligence, her rawness, the way she challenged him. The chemistry they shared felt like a life force separate from them as individuals. None of it made sense. But he wasn't ready for it to end...just yet.

'Okay, so maybe I'm not ready to go back to Monrosa. There's no rush—it's not as if I won't be spending the rest of my life on that island.'

Stamping her feet, she said, 'You make it sound like a prison sentence.' Then with a deep shudder she added, 'It's way too cold out here.'

He followed her back inside and as he closed the door Alice asked, 'What is it about Monrosa that makes you so reluctant to go back there? I know there's the tension with your dad, but it has to be the most beautiful place I have ever visited. Endless sunshine, a rich and fascinating history, incredible beaches and food, and the warmest of people.'

He placed a log on the fire. 'Which is not something that can be said of my father.' He went and sat in the chair he had earlier been seated on. Instead of curling back into her space in the corner of the sofa, Alice sat on the footstool in front of him. She was wearing her black leather mini-skirt again, this time with a soft cream polo-neck jumper and black high heels. She pulled the sleeves of the jumper down over her hands and inched the footstool closer to the fire. He should switch the lights back on, but he liked how the flames of the fire flickered warm light across her face, dancing over the swell of her lips and the prominence of her cheekbones. She smiled at him, a hesitant smile but her eyes held his, an understanding, a recognition, making his heart stumble over in his chest.

'I spoke to your father at Kara's wedding. I liked him. He's blunt. But I prefer that to insincerity and lies.'

'You *liked* him? All my other friends are terrified of him. They try to be polite about it, but I see them slinking out of his way.'

'You know how sometimes you meet someone in life, and you click for some reason, and, as strange as it might sound, I felt that with your dad.' She shrugged. 'Maybe it's because we both use defensiveness to protect ourselves.'

'I would class my father's approach as attack rather than defence.'

'I know things must have been hard... I've been through it with my own dad. Ultimately I had to decide whether to keep working at our relationship or to break all ties. I know that's probably not an option available to you because of your roles and responsibilities, but maybe you need to redefine your expectations of what your father can give you. It may not be what you want and need, but at least you won't be constantly disappointed and hurt. That's what I found the hardest with my dad, the rollercoaster of hoping and expecting something from him, only to be let down.'

'Why should I have to adjust—why should I have to deal with his constant criticism?'

She shrugged. 'If you try to understand why he's so critical it might help you deal with his behaviour. After all, he must be hurting somehow to act this way.'

He sat back in his chair, knowing she was right. But trying to understand his father could mean having to let go of years of anger and frustration on his part. And perhaps even forgiving his father for the isolation and humiliation he had wrought on him. A forgiveness he wasn't sure he was capable of.

'There's more to your reluctance to return to the island than your dad though, isn't there?'

He shook his head. 'No.'

Shifting in her seat, her gaze holding his, she softly said, 'Last year I went back to the town where I grew up. I hadn't been there since my parents separated. I actually felt physically sick. I hadn't expected it, but seeing the town triggered huge panic in me. I couldn't wait to get out of there.'

Luis understood. He didn't experience panic, but he was always cranky and defensive while in Monrosa.

'What one word would you use about how you feel about Monrosa?'

He stared at her, undone by the gentleness in her voice, undone by the wave of grief he didn't even know he held on to. 'Sadness.'

'Because of your mum?'

He closed his eyes, suddenly wanting a drink. Or any other distraction that would serve to get him out of this conversation. He never, ever spoke to anyone about any of this. 'Every time I see the Monrosian coastline as we fly in, for a moment I think my mother will be there. That I will get to hug her again.' He swallowed, a barrel of emotion, of loss and regrets, sitting on his chest. 'I think that I'll be able to tell her one more time how much I love her.' He tried to stop there but it was as though the emotional break he usually had so firmly in place was out of action in the face of Alice's steady gaze. 'For those few moments I don't feel quite so alone.'

She tilted her head, smiled so kindly at him that he was forced to blink hard as tears stung the backs of his eyes. 'I had always thought you were the least alone person on this earth,' she said.

He threw his head back, running a hand through his hair. 'I spend my days trying not to be.'

'Do you like yourself, Luis?'

He shook his head. 'That's way too deep for me.'

She edged ever closer, her knees touching his, a playful smile on her lips. 'Now, don't go telling this to anyone, but I like you. In fact, I think you're pretty incredible. Yes, you need to stop and draw a breath every now and again. And find happiness within yourself. But I know that you're going to go on from here and be a force of good in this world. You have a unique opportunity and position of influence, a unique personality full of energy and optimism. The world needs good guys like you more than ever before.'

His heart turned inside out at her words. She really believed in him. He grinned, trying to regain control of his emotions. 'You're not expecting a lot from me, are you?'

'Nothing that you aren't capable of. Look at the courage and determination it took for you to win the World Series. I reckon you're capable of doing anything you put your mind to.'

'It's easy when you are in a job you love, with a clear goal in sight and surrounded by a brilliant team.'

She shrugged. 'Surround yourself with a new team. I get that transitioning from one life to another is hard, but take time out to understand what it is you actually want to achieve in life.'

What did he want in life? In his twenties he had thrown himself into anything that gave him an adrenaline rush and got him away from Monrosa. And anything that antagonised his father. He grimaced, knowing he had to accept some of the responsibility for his dysfunctional relationship with his father. 'Do you have what you want in life worked out?'

'Kind of. I know I want to create a love for history in students. I have some ideas on writing accessible historical fiction for teenagers focused on real-life events. So often, the way history is taught, teenagers can't relate to it. We can learn so much by the mistakes past generations have made. It frustrates me to see us make the same mistakes time and time again, more often than not allowing fear and ignorance, a narrow world view, to guide our decisions.'

He smiled at the passion in her voice. 'So why are you struggling with your PhD?'

She sighed. 'Good question. I guess that for so long my life has been predictable. I like that order. It makes me feel safe. When I finish my PhD I don't know what my life will look like, what changes I'll have to make.'

'So, I'm heading towards a life filled with

structure and protocol and you're heading into uncertainty—the complete opposites of one another and what neither of us want.'

She tilted her head. 'We could swap. I think I'd love following royal protocol.' She laughed. 'It would suit me perfectly to be surrounded by centuries of history, and there isn't a rebellious bone in my body.'

He ran a hand along his neck. 'Don't say that within earshot of my father at the New Year's Eve ball or he'll try setting you up with me or Ivo—he's keen for us to marry too.'

'Of course I wouldn't! I wasn't implying...' She paused, her forehead puckering. 'Wait, I haven't said that I will go with you to the ball anyway. And there's no way I'm ever marrying, so you're safe on that front. I still can't believe Kara agreed to it in the first place.'

Picking up his phone, he opened up the photo gallery and showed the photograph Edwin had sent to him that morning, of him and Kara happily surrounded by the group of local children who as per tradition visited the palace on Christmas Eve to receive Christmas gifts. 'And look at how happy they are now.'

She studied the photo in silence. 'They really are in love, aren't they?'

He nodded. 'It looks that way...maybe starting as friends is a good place to begin a relationship.'

She gave him an uncertain look. And no wonder. He wasn't even sure himself why he had said that. He needed to lighten the mood. Rapidly. 'Come to the ball with me. It's always a spectacular event but this year it will be even more incredible because Kara is organising it and the proceeds will be going to her charity. She has doubled the numbers attending, and there will not only be the ball, but also an amusement fair, an aerial acrobatics team, a casino... She wants to make it into a huge fundraising event with guests coming from all over the world. Who knows, even you might enjoy it?'

She gave him an evil stare. 'Are you implying that I can be a grumpy pants?'

He laughed. 'Now, why would I ever have reason to think that?'

She studied him closely, as though trying to work him out. 'Tell me the real reason you want me to go to the ball with you—you know that it will raise eyebrows with your family and the media. Why risk endless and incorrect speculation?'

Because I want to dance with you. I want to hear your laughter when I drag you onto an

*amusement ride. I want your calmness. I want
to be with you.*

What was happening to him? Why was he
feeling all these things?

He went to make a quip, intending to say that
she could be his decoy around his father, but
instead he answered, 'Because it's time that I
started creating new memories in Monrosa.'

CHAPTER EIGHT

ALICE RAN OUT of the bathroom and scrambled through her suitcase. Underwear. Make-up bag. She scrambled even more. Where was her roll-up bag of make-up and hairbrushes? Oh, somebody please tell her she hadn't left them sitting on the bathroom counter of her bedroom in Verbier.

She checked her phone. She had forty minutes to get ready. Forty minutes! Her hair alone took nearly that long to dry...so not for the first time she cursed its thick length. She was going to look an absolute mess. At the New Year's Eve ball that the whole of Europe was talking about...according to her mum anyway. But it must be a big deal, given the amount of media parked outside the main gates.

She winced, remembering her mother's shock when she had rung and told her that she was going to the ball, but thankfully she seemed to believe her explanation that Kara wanted some support.

She felt so far out of her depth it wasn't funny. And Luis's father's reproachful look when they had rushed into the palace only fifteen minutes ago hadn't helped.

Giving up on her search for the make-up bag, she ran back into the dressing room to check that she hadn't imagined things when she had briefly looked in there before her rushed shower. The five exquisite ballgowns were still there, hanging on the rail—waiting for her to decide which one to wear tonight. Despite her protests that it was unnecessary, Luis had insisted on ordering a selection of gowns for her to choose from. She lifted a sleek beaded turquoise dress from the rail and placed it against her. It was beautiful…and tiny. Would she even fit into it? Had Luis given the designer the wrong measurements? Or maybe it was she who had got the measurements wrong in the first place. Which was no wonder, given her distraction thanks to Luis standing behind her, his hands on her hips and his lips on her neck, whispering a long list of things he wanted to find out about her body as she had struggled to write down her measurements. They had spent the last five days snowboarding…and making out. On the slopes, in the pool, in the sauna, on the sofa. Just about everywhere, to be frank. It had been exhilarating. Passionate. All-consuming. Unstoppable. She simply couldn't get enough of him. She craved his touch, the pressure of his body against hers.

Every morning when they met for breakfast he pulled her into a bear hug, and as his arms wrapped around her and she inhaled the citrus smell from his recently showered skin she'd place her head against his chest and hear the thump of his heart and a sense of peace would wash over her. And then he would kiss her. And that peace would be replaced with heat. A heat that would only grow throughout the day until in the darkness of the night, as he stood outside her bedroom door, which he insisted on walking her to every single night, they would make out like teenagers. Hot, lusty kisses. Intimate touches. He gave her the teenage passion she had been too scared to experience when she'd actually been a teenager.

'What is the matter with you?'

She could still hear the disdain in Rory's voice the one time they had come close to making love. The implication that she was damaged. She had panicked at the last moment and had leapt away from him, pulling her jeans and top back on as Rory stared at her with impatient and angry disbelief. Her dad's abuse had been too raw and recent. She had been too bruised to let anyone get close to her.

The passage of time and Luis's kindness, not to mention the chemistry between them, were all lowering the defences she had put around herself, and every night when she reluctantly shut her bedroom door to him she had battled with the urge to swing the door open again and beg him to sleep with her. Mostly pride holding her back. But also, just about enough sense to realise that in essence what was happening between them was nothing other than a short holiday fling.

Reckoning the turquoise dress wouldn't fit her, she checked each of the other dresses. The silver dress was equally tiny, the white sheath with a gold belt not her colour. Which left a full-skirted red dress and a jade-green fishtail dress. The red dress looked the most likely to fit her.

Back in the bedroom she pulled the towel from around her head, her wet hair falling around her shoulders. She jumped at a knock on the door. Gingerly opening it, she gave a cry of relief. 'Kara!'

Kara swept into the room, carrying the long

train of her gold sequinned dress. Kara went to hug her, but Alice ducked out of the way. 'No! I'll ruin your hair and make-up.' Stepping back, she shook her head. 'You look like a million dollars.'

Kara grinned. 'My hair and make-up team are miracle-workers.' Then, pulling Alice into a hug, despite her protests, she added, 'It's so good to see you. I was really worried your flight wouldn't be able to take off because of the snowstorm.'

Extracting herself from the hug, Alice pointed to her hair. 'I need to get this dry. And do my make-up… I'd like to say that I'm not panicking but I am.'

'My team should still be in the palace—I'll call them.'

Alice sighed in relief. 'That would be amazing, thank you.'

'Deal—but you have to tell me first, though, what's going on between you and Luis.'

'There's nothing going on between us.' Seeing Kara's disbelieving expression, Alice went and opened one of the shoeboxes sitting on the ottoman at the bottom of her bed. 'He got it into his head that I needed minding over Christmas. We get on. But that's all. We're complete opposites. Now seriously, can you go and call your team? I'm never going to be ready at this rate.'

'I'd never have put the two of you together, but the more Edwin and I discussed it, the more I realised that you are really suited. You balance each other out perfectly and you're actually not that different.'

Lifting a red sandal from the box, which must have been sent to match the red gown, she waved it at Kara. 'I have my make-up to do, I have to squeeze myself into a dress and hope that these sandals fit me... I don't have time to be chatting about a hypothetical relationship with Luis that's never going to happen. And for the record, he's an extroverted risk-taking prince and I'm a history student who struggles in a room with more than ten people.'

'Yes, but you are both incredibly intelligent, kind and compassionate.' Pausing, Kara considered her for a moment. 'Luis called Edwin yesterday to schedule a meeting tomorrow between him, Edwin and their father to discuss what his role will be when he returns to Monrosa. It's the first time that he's been willing to discuss his return. Edwin needs his support, so it's a huge relief for us—and I can't help but think that you've played a role in him taking this step. So isn't it any wonder that I reckon that there's a whole lot more going on between you two than either of you are letting on?'

Alice grabbed her phone and checked the time. 'I have half an hour to get ready. Can you please go and find your team?' Seeing that Kara wasn't about to budge, she added as way of a bribe, 'If you do, I promise that I'll take part in your mud-run fundraiser next year.'

'As long as you promise to persuade Luis to also take part,' Kara replied with a cheeky smile before disappearing out of the door.

Tugging off her towel, Alice pulled on a white lace thong and the dressing gown she had found in the bathroom. The red sandals consisted of endless rows of tiny straps, so, sitting on the ottoman, she undid the top five straps of each sandal before stepping into them, and cursed at how tricky it was to tie them back up.

Wrangling with the straps, she called, 'Come in,' when there was another knock on the door. 'That was quick…' She stopped, her heart missing a beat. Standing at the doorway, freshly showered and dressed in black tie, Luis let his gaze drop down to her sandals.

'Need some help?'

Before she was able to decline his offer he was already kneeling before her, his hand reaching for an ankle. He tied the straps in silence. A heated charge filled the room. She had sworn to herself this very morning that once they were in Monrosa everything would change—that she would stop being so aware of him, stop falling to pieces whenever they were in the same room.

His hands ran up the length of her calves, his eyes meeting hers. 'Great sandals.'

Such simple words but said with such heat and meaning, and they were followed up with him kissing her briefly but passionately on the mouth. And when he pulled back the intimacy in his eyes sent flutters of exhilaration and panic through her.

She was getting way too addicted to him. She knew it. She really, really was trying to fight it. But she might as well have been trying to hold back the tide.

'I'm supposed to be getting ready.'

'I think you look pretty great as you are.'

Yeah, right. Wet hair. No make-up. A fluffy dressing gown that made her look like a polar bear. But... Luis looked as though he truly meant it.

He reached into his inner pocket. 'I have a surprise for you.'

She groaned. 'Not another one.' Last night he had taken her to a local outdoor ice rink that was rather embarrassingly holding a date night. Not only had she had to endure the humiliation of having to cling to Luis for the night, but their slow movements around the ice had been accompanied by the most romantic playlist known to mankind.

From his pocket he pulled out a yellow and green ointment tube and held it out to her.

Puzzled, she picked it up.

'For all of your bruises—it's produced on the island and is famed for its healing properties.'

'Is this an apology for showing off on the ice last night and tripping me up in the process?'

He took the tube from her with a wry smile. Undoing the cap, he smeared some of the cream onto his finger and rubbed it onto the bruise on her knee. And then he parted her dressing gown, exposing more of her thighs. She knew she should protest, grab the ointment from him, but instead she watched with hypnotic fascination as he gently worked the ointment into every visible bruise, most of them a result of her poor attempts to learn to snowboard. Her heart dipped and soared, tongues of fire licked her insides and her poor brain tried its best to be heard amongst all that chaos, warning her that things were really getting out of control.

His thumb flicked over the lace panel of her

thong. The tongues of fire burnt even more brightly. His head dropped down, his tongue trailing against her inner thigh. She threw her head back, all thought closing down as she became consumed with the sensation of his tongue, flicking against the fabric of her underwear. She grappled for some coherent thoughts. 'I need…to get ready…this isn't fair.'

He gently bit into the inner skin of her thigh. She yelped, not in pain but because it felt so good.

With a self-satisfied smile he popped the top back on the ointment and reached inside his pocket again. This time he pulled out another white velvet box from Jarrad Jewellers.

She eyed it warily.

'I'd like you to wear them tonight.' When she didn't take the box he added softly, 'It's a thank-you for coming to Monrosa with me… it's made the journey home easier.'

Her heart tightened. She blinked against a stinging sensation at the backs of her eyes. 'I'm glad.'

Opening the box, she inhaled sharply at the exquisite beauty of what lay within. 'Earrings to match the necklace you gave me on Christmas Day.'

'Jarrad's couriered it here today.'

Taking the box from her, he came and sat beside her and, taking one of the earrings out, pulled back the clasp and gently placed it on her earlobe.

'You noticed that I don't have my ears pierced.' Why was that fact so important, so bittersweet?

He placed the other earring on her other lobe, the soft wool of his dress jacket rubbing against her cheek. And then, holding her head so tenderly that she barely felt the pressure of his hands, he placed a kiss on each earlobe. 'I have to go and receive our guests with the rest of my family. I've asked a friend, Henri, to escort you to the ball. He will be waiting for you in the Blue Room downstairs.'

She nodded, and after one final kiss goodbye he left. She needed to get up, make sure she could walk in the sandals. But instead she collapsed back onto the bed behind the ottoman, exhausted by sexual frustration and by the knowledge that tomorrow she had to say goodbye to this Christmas tale. A tale, like all other Christmas tales, that was full of marvels and miracles but had no place in the real world.

Luis entered the ballroom and scanned the room for a red dress. He circled the room, waving to friends and associates but moving on, not stopping to chat, his eyes darting across the crowded dance floor. He came to a stop. A man was holding a woman in a red dress way too closely. He cursed as the man's hands ran over the pale skin of her bare back. He moved towards them but then the crowd parted, and he realised it wasn't Alice after all.

He left the ballroom, thrown by his jealousy and how desperately he wanted to track Alice down. He wanted to be with her. They hadn't spoken all evening. They had been seated at different tables during dinner and he had spent the entire meal juggling entertaining a sports-obsessed multinational CEO while trying to ignore the frostiness of his father, who had been seated next to him, and keeping an eye on Alice, seated to the side of the room.

By the end of the meal he had managed to convince the CEO that he should consider using the conference and sporting facilities on Monrosa for corporate events...and had developed an irritating crick in his neck from checking on Alice.

She had sat at her table, her reserve, the quiet way she occupied a space, so endearing, so positively Alice that he had wanted to stroll over to her and tell her just how amazing she truly was. Watching her from afar, he had wanted to turn to his father and tell him about the incredible person he had spent the last few days with. He had wanted to tell him about her determination to learn to snowboard, how at times tears of frustration had misted her eyes, but she had refused to give up. He had wanted to tell him of his pride in watching her complete a run. He had wanted to tell him about how they had talked about his future, how she had helped him move closer to identifying a new purpose in life, her intelligent questions, her constant positivity and belief in him enabling him to begin the process of deciding on what he wanted to achieve. He had wanted to tell his father how they had spent hours talking over their meals, something he had never been capable of before, always too restless, too uncomfortable in his own skin.

Now, out in the corridor, moving away from the sound of the orchestra in the ballroom, he took out his phone and began to dial Alice's number, but outside the library he came to a stop. Her back to him, Alice was pulling a book from a high-up shelf. Her hair was tied up into a loose bun. The strapless dress was cut low at the back, exposing the delicate workings of her shoulder blades and the neat, fragile bumps of her spine. The skirt of the gown, embellished with crystals, glittered in the low lights of the library.

He stepped inside. 'I'm glad you're continuing to take my advice to wear red,' he growled, remembering her cry earlier, how her legs had trembled uncontrollably as he had kissed and caressed her thighs. He pushed away the thought that what they were doing, the constant kisses and touches, the endless caressing and teasing, were almost more intimate than actually sleeping together.

She whipped around, blushing. 'I look like a Christmas decoration.'

Somebody chuckled behind him. With a start he spun around to find his father sitting on a sofa. Alice went and sat on the sofa opposite him. Both Alice and his father looked to him, waiting for him to say something.

He backed towards the door. 'I just came to see if you're okay and apologise for not spending time with you—Kara asked me to go and speak to the staff from her new offices in Sri Lanka and Auckland. They are rolling out a peer programme in both countries and it was encouraging to hear about the impact it is already having.' He came to a stop, feeling crazily emotional remembering some of the stories he had heard from the staff of teenagers alone and isolated, struggling with mental-health issues. He cleared his throat, hating to feel so vulnerable in front of his father. He looked at Alice. 'I need to go and speak to the guests in the ballroom; do join me when you are free.'

Alice patted the space beside her. 'Why don't you come and chat with us for five minutes first?'

His father sat back in his seat and studied him. It would be so much easier to go back to the ballroom. Be distracted by light-hearted chat and banter. Have a few drinks.

Alice's gaze met his and with the slightest of nods she silently said, *This is the right thing to do.*

He went and sat beside her. Alice smiled in his father's direction. 'Your father, His Highness, very kindly has been giving me an outline of your family history.' She threw him a teasing look. 'You're descended from warrior kings—no wonder you need to have challenges in your life.'

His father made a disapproving sound. Alice turned her attention back to him. 'You must be proud of Luis winning the World Series.'

His father mumbled something that was indecipherable.

'Did you ever go and watch one of his races?'

Luis stared at Alice. Where was she going with this?

'I was never invited.'

He stared at his father. 'I never thought you'd want to come.'

His father gave an indignant snort. 'Of course I would have liked to see you race—if I had been asked.'

He couldn't believe this. 'Why didn't you come anyway?'

His father's nostrils flared. 'You didn't want me there.'

'I never said that.'

His father gave a bitter laugh. 'You never said anything to me, full stop.'

Luis sat forward in his seat, anger and disbelief firing inside of him. 'That's because you stole all of the airtime criticising me.'

His father's mouth hardened. And then with a jolt of shock he realised that there were tears in his father's eyes. His father looked at Alice and then at him, as if deciding whether to respond. Eventually he said, 'Did you have to pick such a dangerous sport? And not just that—after your mother died, why did you insist on riding her horse? Even though I had banned you from doing so?'

He closed his eyes. 'It wasn't Cassini's fault; something caused him to bolt. Mum adored him. She'd have wanted us to care for him. She certainly wouldn't have wanted you to sell him.'

'I had no option but to sell him when you kept defying my orders.'

About to fire back a furious retort, he felt Alice's hand touch his thigh and he swallowed his words.

'Can you understand how difficult it was for me to see you riding him?'

He winced at the pain in his father's voice and quietly admitted, 'I hadn't realised... I wasn't thinking about you.'

He waited for his father to deliver some barbed comment, point out just how selfish and irresponsible he was, but instead his father asked quietly, 'Are you returning to powerboating—is that why you want to speak to Edwin and me tomorrow?'

Should he say yes, that he was going back to the life and career he loved? Beside him Alice shifted, the red material of her skirt landing to cover one of his knees. The past few days with her, the intimacy, the calmness of his days, how much he had wanted to find her just now—all of a sudden he was no longer certain the life he thought he loved so much was all that he really thought it was.

'I'm not sure… I want to discuss it with you and Edwin tomorrow.'

His father stood. 'Edwin needs your help—the role of monarch is becoming ever more demanding in the changing global environment.' He moved towards the door but before he left he added, 'And Edwin is right—it's time that we became a family again.' With a nod in Alice's direction he said, 'It's been nice to see you again, Alice; please come back and see us some time soon.'

They sat in silence, Luis's father's footsteps out in the corridor fading away.

'He likes you.'

She considered him. 'Why do you say that?'

'He doesn't usually speak to people outside his inner circle.'

Alice considered that for a moment. 'I think he was just looking for an excuse to get away from the ballroom—the music is pretty loud.'

'How did you both end up speaking in the first place?'

She laughed at his puzzlement. 'I just went over and started chatting to him; he looked bored.' She stopped and gasped. 'Did I just commit some social faux pas in approaching him?'

Luis grinned. 'Perhaps…but the fact that he remembered your name means you're forgiven in his eyes.'

Confused, she asked, 'What's the significance of him remembering my name?'

'He deliberately calls people by the wrong name when he's unhappy with them.' Leaning his head against the back of the sofa, he added on a sigh, 'I had no idea that he wanted me to invite him to my races…' He looked in her direction. 'Am I right in thinking he was saying that he was worried about my safety?'

She nodded.

Sitting upright, he took her hand in his. 'I'm sorry you had to sit through that conversation, and that I've spent so little time with you tonight.'

Threading her fingers through his, she answered truthfully, 'I hope things work out for you, Luis—that the differences in your family can be healed and that you find a career that will fulfil and challenge you.'

'I'm glad you're here.'

Her heart melted at the tenderness in his voice. 'I'm glad I'm here too.' But then, trying to gather herself, remembering that tomorrow she would have to go back to reality, she forced herself to smile and added, 'It's not often that I'll get to wear a designer dress and hang out with A-list celebrities. I can't wait to see Toni's expression when I tell her.'

Standing, he helped her up and with the sexiest of grins asked, 'Have you ever danced with a prince at a ball?'

She smiled. 'No, I can't say that I have.'

He led her to the ballroom, where elaborate cascades of white flowers hung from the ceiling, filling the room with a delicate floral scent. The lights were down low, and the orchestra was playing a slow number. They moved onto the dance floor, Luis saying hello to everyone they passed, and as they danced he continued to acknowledge those around them. But between them there was a private dance going on. Every touch, every look held a significance. His fingers ran down her spine. Hers touched the cords of his neck. His mouth beside her ear, he whispered, 'As much as I love that dress, I have to admit I can't help but fantasise about you wearing those sandals and nothing else.'

She blushed at the sensuous tone in his voice. But then frustration and bewilderment that these were their last hours together had her step away and say, 'Follow me.'

She led him out onto the terrace, heading in the direction of the bright lights of the Ferris wheel. But that was not her destination. Instead, she led him off the path and into a copse of trees, walking until they could go no further.

She backed him up against a tree trunk. And admitted, 'There never was a dare.'

He raised an eyebrow, waiting for her to further explain her confession.

'That first time I kissed you, here in the palace...nobody dared me. But I had to do it, I had to kiss you. I had never met someone I so badly wanted to kiss in my entire life. And it had nothing to do with your beard.' Desire was stripping away her every inhibition. She didn't care about the past or the future. For the next few hours she wanted to be truly alive. She wanted to forget every reason why this was a bad idea and live within this man's skin. She wanted to know every part of him.

He considered her words. Nodded sombrely. 'Thank you for sharing that with me.'

'I want to kiss you again.'

'No.'

She blinked. No! What did he mean? They had been making out for the past week.

His arm reaching around her waist, he

whipped her around so that it was her back to the tree. The bark was smooth and warm. Monrosa was a long way away from the crisp coldness of Verbier and the dampness of London.

He placed a hand on the trunk, hit her with a dark look. 'This time, I'm the one doing the kissing. But be warned…it will be nothing like your kiss. This kiss…is going to be demanding and hard,' he paused, his mouth reaching for her ear, 'and perhaps even a little brutal.'

Her heart thumped against her chest. She was scared, but in a totally sensual way.

His eyes flashed. 'So, do you want me to kiss you?'

She nodded, her heart beating even faster.

His finger resting at the base of her throat for a moment, he traced a slow path down over her necklace and into the valley of her breasts.

Her back arched.

His mouth touched her neck. She inhaled the earthy tones of his aftershave, her head spinning as his mouth moved up her throat in a slow, tortuous path.

When his mouth reached hers, he drew back and whispered, 'You're extraordinary,' and then his lips were on hers. Soft. Light.

She moaned. 'You said it would be brutal.'

'Patience,' he whispered back.

His mouth parted hers. She gasped at the wonder of the heat of his mouth. One hand was on her waist, the other running over the outline of her breast, sending pulses of pleasure the length of her body.

His tongue touched hers, but it was all too teasing, too light.

She panted out, 'More. Harder.'

He pulled back. 'Are you sure?'

She nodded. His expression hardened with dark passion. His mouth found hers again. Demanding and in control, deep and seeking, sending a feverish heat through her. His hands wrapped around her wrists, drawing her arms above her head, and he pinned them to the trunk with one hand. Her body arched into the rigid planes of his. Her head spun. His mouth continued to wreak havoc on hers.

She arched even more when his free hand tugged down the front of her dress. She gasped as her nipples felt the warm air of the night. Her legs buckled when his mouth left hers and, dipping down, his lips slowly circled over her breast in ever-decreasing circles of tender kisses until his tongue grazed over her nipple. She cried out, her body buckling, needing the pressure of his weight, needing him. His mouth sucked on her nipple. She writhed, wanting to free her arms, wanting to touch him. He applied more pressure with his mouth. She gasped. His free hand touched her other nipple. She was already about to come apart.

'I want you... I need you tonight, Luis,' she whispered.

For a moment she thought he hadn't heard her, but, lifting his head, he drew her dress back up over her breasts and he gently released her arms. He let out a sigh, touched his hand to her cheek, the passion in his eyes softening. He looked at her with such tenderness that she wanted to scream.

'I would like that more than anything in this world, but it would be wrong—'

She interrupted him, undone by his gentleness, 'Why? Why would it be wrong?' She stopped and let out a bitter laugh. 'Or am I getting what happens between us every single time we're in each other's company wrong?'

He considered her for a moment before asking, 'Why now?'

Desire and emotion had her speak without thinking. 'Because I know we have no future but that doesn't mean we can't have now. Because I'm about to explode with frustration and I'm so turned on by you that I actually want to cry.' She pushed away from the tree, her heart beating, beating, beating against her chest, and added, 'Because you make me feel safe.'

She moved to the edge of the copse but before she walked out into the open she turned and glanced at Luis. Her heart sank. He was watching her with concern, all evidence of passion and desire erased from his expression.

CHAPTER NINE

LUIS CURSED AS Lars Hendrick, an old university friend, potted the black. Placing the billiard cue back in the rack, he doled out his bet to a grinning Lars. Following the midnight fireworks the ball had ended over an hour ago and, as per tradition, all the diehard partygoers had decamped to the games rooms to continue the party with more dancing and drinking. He looked around at those out on the temporary dance floor and the loud groups chatting animatedly. He should go and join them. But instead he hung back.

Alice had said goodnight to him the moment the ball had ended. After their kiss in the woods he had caught up with her and persuaded her to ride the Ferris wheel with him, and then they had danced together again. And the whole performance had turned him inside out.

He wanted to lie naked next to her. Worship her body. But what if he hurt her?

He thought back to her gentle presence when he had spoken to his father earlier. His heart tightened. He had never thought to invite his father to his races. He had assumed he wouldn't want to attend. But what if the real truth of not inviting him was more to do with how frightened he was that his father would throw the invite in his face? Ever since his mother had died and his father had grown angry and detached, he had been waiting and fearing his rejection. And a self-perpetuating cycle of behaviour had evolved between them where he would make a preventive strike to either force his father's hand to push him away, or he would close down, not allowing his father any opportunity to hurt him.

The voices and music around him faded into the background as his mind became a whirl of uncomfortable thoughts. He went to the bar and fixed himself a whiskey. He didn't want to hurt Alice by sleeping with her. But what if there was more to it than that? What if he was scared of laying his soul on the line by sleeping with her, only to have her walk away?

He closed his eyes. Rocked by his own thoughts. He opened them again, knowing that the sensible thing to do was to go out onto the dance floor and lose himself in the music and the meaningless chatter. Once again, he should run away from everything inside of him.

But instead he pushed his untouched drink away and went and climbed the stairs to the guest wing.

He stood outside her door, wondering if he should wait until morning. He was terrified. Terrified of getting this all wrong. He undid his bow tie, opened the collar of his shirt. His rational self knew that he shouldn't be here. But his heart knew the truth. No doubt others would tell him that he was crazy, that there was no way he could feel this way so quickly. That he was only confusing his feelings for Alice with lust. He ran a hand through his hair. Dragged in a long, slow breath. And knocked on her door.

Minutes passed before she eventually answered. He took in the *Our lace* jersey she had changed into, her scrubbed face and the toothbrush in her hand.

She backed away, allowing him to enter. She touched the jersey. 'I was about to go to bed...'

He wanted to take her in his arms, kiss away the beads of water lingering on her hairline from washing her face. And no matter just how adorable she looked in the soccer jersey, he wanted to lift it over her head and see for the very first time her naked body. And, despite the desperate build-up in his body, he knew he would control it enough to make love to her slowly and tenderly, needing to show her how much he worshipped her.

But there were things he needed to say first. He gestured for her to sit on the bed and he pulled a low antique bedroom chair in front of her and sat too.

She sat looking at him, her eyes wide, the colour in her cheeks draining.

This clearly wasn't what she was expecting.

A whoosh of affection for her stole his words away. He touched his hand against her bare knee. He cursed once again at the large bruise on her thigh. He placed his hand over it, wanting to heal it.

He needed to talk, tell her. For a person whose school reports always contained the feedback, *Luis needs to stop talking and concentrate more,* and who spent his days constantly chatting, only now did he realise how little he actually said. In the past week he had spoken more honestly than he had done in his lifetime. But now, facing her, gaze to gaze, the hard shell of his true feelings cracked open— to actually share them with her felt like stepping into an abyss.

She pulled back from him, her expression

growing wary. He opened his mouth, wondering what on earth he was doing. 'I want us to make love…'

She frowned. 'Well, it sure doesn't—'

He interrupted her, 'I know I'm messing this up, but there's something you need to know first.'

She sighed. 'There's another woman, isn't there?' She said it in a teasing tone, the accusation of the past no longer there, but clearly wanting to defuse the tension between them as much as he wanted to.

'You well know that there isn't.' He was finding it impossible to breathe. 'Before we make love, I want you to know that I'm in love with you and want us to be together, to be in a relationship.'

Alice laughed. She could hear herself. She knew she should stop but something had gone wrong in her brain. A defence mechanism of some sort had gone into overdrive.

Luis was staring at her, perplexed.

No, don't look confused. Don't look hurt. Don't look as though you actually meant those words. You can't love me. You simply can't. This is all too much. Too fast. Why are you telling me that you love me? What's really behind those words? My dad would yank my mum's hair until she screamed, punch her, threaten her, but then when the fury subsided he would hold her and plead his love. I don't want to hear that you love me because I might believe you and give you my heart, only for you to destroy it. This isn't what was supposed to happen. Laugh with me. Tell me you were only kidding.

But he didn't. And she blurted out, 'Don't be ridiculous, of course you don't love me.'

His head jerked. As though she had slapped him. 'Why would I say it if I didn't mean it?'

Panic had her ask, 'Have you been drinking?'

He sat back in his chair, his expression turning to granite. 'No.'

Alice jumped off the bed. She paced the room, trying not to give in to the temptation of opening the bedroom door and bolting. 'You don't love me, Luis…' She waved vaguely between them, attempted a smile. 'What we have is lust and chemistry.'

She waited for him to smile back and agree. She waited for him to make this simple and uncomplicated. Why couldn't they just sleep together like other people? Why couldn't they just revel in the physical, the passion of deep attraction?

But instead, his expression proud, he asked quietly, 'Why don't you believe me?'

She threw her hands into the air. 'Why don't I believe you? Because you don't really mean it. You can't. You're telling me that you love me and want to be in a relationship despite having previously told me that you wanted to remain single.' She paused, and looked at him for long seconds, wondering if she knew him at all. 'Or am I giving too much significance to that word love? Perhaps you use it easily. Perhaps you have said it to every woman you have slept with.'

He walked to her bedroom window. She hadn't pulled the curtains and had opened the window, wanting to sleep to the sound of the nearby sea. He stared out into the darkness for a moment before turning and regarding her, his expression still as hard as stone. And she was reminded that he was descended from proud warrior kings. 'You are the first woman I have ever said those words to.'

She closed her eyes, trying to take a hold of the hot panic running through her. Love was fickle and manipulative. She had had a childhood of witnessing how it could be turned on you, how your love could be used as a weapon to destroy you. She opened her eyes. 'You don't love me. You're looking for something to take the place of the career and life you're leaving. You're looking for something that will take the sting of returning to Monrosa away. You're looking for a new distraction. And that distraction just happens to be me.'

White noise crowded Luis's head.

She doesn't believe me. She doesn't believe me.

'Do you trust in anything that I say?'

She folded her arms, her expression shut off. 'Now... I'm not sure.'

His throat tightened. He should walk away. While he still had some dignity. But questions burned inside of him. 'What has the past week been to you...has it meant anything?'

She backed away. 'This is too much. I thought we were friends; I don't know how to cope with this.'

'Is that all you thought we had—friendship?' He stalked the room, adrenaline pounding through him.

She rounded on him. 'What do you want me to say?' She gestured vaguely between them. 'Why are you rushing this...why are you rushing me? Why are you backing me into a corner?'

He had to get out. Now. Before he said anything else. Shame was creeping along his veins, shutting down his capacity to think. 'Forget that I said anything.'

She dropped her hands. 'Oh, Luis, why did you have—?'

He cut across her. 'You're leaving tomorrow?'

He didn't know himself if that was a question or a statement.

She looked at him with a helpless expression. 'That's what was planned.'

He nodded. 'It's for the best.' It felt as though he was watching himself from a distance. The pain inside of him shutting down everything but a forceful need to protect himself.

Alice watched Luis walk to the door, place his hand on the door handle.

Go. Give me some space.

She wanted to crawl into bed and hide under the bedclothes the way she had used to as a child to drown out her parents' arguments. She longed for a dark, warm space where she wasn't under attack. She wanted to curl herself into a tight ball and hum. Calm the panic that was crowding her head.

His hand twisted the handle.

No! Don't go. I'm sorry. I believe you. But am I crazy to even think that? I want to believe that you do love me. I want to trust you. I want to trust myself... I think I've fallen in love with you too. But is all this misguided, so full of misjudgement and crossed purposes, all so rushed and forced that we'll only hurt one another?

He opened the door. Looked back in her direction. As though waiting for her to say something. But no words would come to her. She was frozen by indecision and the fear that she was being used and manipulated.

He closed the door, his expression rigid. Tears burned the backs of her eyes. What had she done?

CHAPTER TEN

THE WINE BAR door opened, letting in a blast of icy air. Alice craned to see if it was Toni but let out a disappointed breath when she saw that it was a group of office workers. She checked her phone. Nothing. She settled back into her seat, still pretending to be checking for messages and not unintentionally listening in to the conversations of the couples seated either side of her. She sipped her coffee. And tried to process the fact that she had done it. She had submitted her thesis that very afternoon. She still had the last hurdle of the PhD defence presentation to face in a few months' time, but for now she was going to celebrate.

Her phone pinged.

A message from Toni appeared on the screen. She was still in London. She had missed her flight to Dublin. Concerned, Alice typed back a message, asking if everything was okay. Toni messaged back saying that she was stuck in work and couldn't talk but that she was so sorry to let her down.

Leaving the bar, Alice shivered at the biting wind. She had managed to lose her new red hat somewhere in the university and her coat was no defence against the arctic cold sweeping through the streets of Dublin.

A celebration party in honour of Luis's championship win was taking place right now. Alice ducked her head down, fighting to walk into the unrelenting wind. Had it been sunny in Monrosa today? Would they still have daylight? Kara had sent her an invite. She had been taken aback by just how happy she had been that Luis's win was being celebrated in Monrosa…and how desperately sad she was that she wouldn't be there. For a few hours she had contemplated accepting the invite but in the end she had messaged her apologies to Kara, not wanting to take away from the day for Luis…and not sure she could handle seeing him again.

She missed him. Despite having buried herself in her PhD for every waking moment, she missed him with every fibre of her being. She missed his smiles, the way he stirred her tea. She missed catching him regarding her with what seemed like open affection and fondness. She missed the feel of his hand cradling the back of her head when he hugged her. Was that what being in love meant? Missing the other person so deeply you felt as though you had lost yourself? Waking in the middle of the night thinking you heard their voice whispering something to you? She didn't know what love was. Her dad had said he loved her mum. And she had so desperately wanted to believe him. She had wanted to believe that things would get better, that they could be a family. But her dad had used their love and turned it on them, crushing their hopes and dreams. What if Luis really did love her, for now, but what if that changed? What if he stopped loving her? What if he left her with all the scars of panic and zero self-esteem that her mum was still battling?

The entrance door to her apartment block was sticking again and it took her ages to force it open. Inside she gathered up a scattering of mail, which one of her fellow apartment-block dwellers had clearly stepped on, given the boot-shaped imprint that was across some of the envelopes.

She spotted his envelope immediately. It wasn't hard. The heavy cream paper was in stark contrast to the cheap white envelopes from various banks and telecom companies.

She studied the handwriting, the same large, looping letters that she had first seen on the gift card attached to his Christmas present to her. Would she ever find peace? Would her life ever stop feeling so empty? One day, would she learn to face the future with enthusiasm again? Would colour replace the now constant greyness?

Her studio apartment was like an icebox. She checked her boiler and as she suspected the water pressure had dropped again and it was out of action. She topped it up, knowing she should contact her landlord to complain but she didn't have the energy.

Coat still on, she opened the fridge and shut it. From upstairs came footsteps and muffled music and laughter. The girls who shared the apartment were getting ready for a night out. There went her night's sleep.

She contemplated ringing her mum for a chat but instead switched on a side lamp, flicked off all the other lights in the room and collapsed onto her bed.

When would the feeling of numbness leave her? It was six weeks since she had last seen Luis and it felt as though she was living life in a daze. She had somehow miraculously managed to finish her thesis and not get fired from her job, but it felt as though she was sleepwalking through life.

She missed him. It felt as if a part of her was missing. She missed his touches, his laughter, his teasing, his energy, his kindness. But had all those things been real? Had they all been an act, a way of distracting him from his own life? She rolled onto her side, curling her legs up. Had he been using her…perhaps not even consciously? Maybe he had somehow misguidedly convinced himself that he loved her…but that wouldn't have stopped him from breaking her heart at some point.

Her eyes settled on the pile of cream envelopes peeking out from the top of her kitchen cupboards. She should put the newest one up there…but that meant dragging out a chair to reach the top. The reason why she had stashed them there in the first place was that if they were easy to get to then in a moment of weakness she would succumb to reading them.

What was she going to do with them? She had said she would decide once she had submitted her thesis. Including today's letter there were seven letters in total. If she binned them, she could move on with her life. She closed her eyes. But would she always be haunted by not knowing what was in them?

Seven letters. It had to mean something that he had taken the time to write them all to her.

She dragged out the kitchen chair, climbed up and took the letters down. Sitting on the sofa, she placed his newest letter to the back of the pile. They were all now in date order. She pulled the first letter open.

She read it. Checked the envelope to see if she had missed a page. And then read his brief one-page letter again. Dated just under a month ago, it described a trek he had taken with Edwin and Kara into the mountains of Monrosa. And that was all. She opened the next letter. This letter described his agreement with Edwin and his father as to what his new role would be. She nodded as she read the letter, seeing what a good fit his appointment as Chair of Monrosian Sports and Tourism was. The third and fourth letters described his travels throughout Europe as he promoted Monrosa and spoke at mental-health conferences about the benefits of sport and exercise to well-being. She was happy for him. She really was. But not once did he talk about them…about their week together. Sure, he asked how she was, asked if she would write to him, but apart from that, these letters were distant. Why had he even written them in the first place?

She ripped the fifth letter open. Irritated. Disappointed.

What did you want, Alice? Did you really expect them to be love letters? Letters begging to see you again?

She took the letter out of the envelope, a photograph falling onto her lap. And her heart melted. It was a photo of Luis with the cutest ever dachshund. His letter said that he had adopted him from a local shelter and that his name was Elfo. She stared at the photograph. Stared at him, the man who had insisted on staying in London to keep her company. The man who had made her laugh, sigh, feel more alive than she had ever done in her entire life. She stared at the photo and wondered if somebody was capable of pretending care, kindness and generosity to the level he had, without the mask of pretence slipping? She stared at his photo, tears blurring her vision. She was in love with him. She was in love with him for everything that was magnificent about him. But she still didn't know if his love for her was real.

She opened the next letter. Tears blurred her eyes again when she read about the meeting he'd attended in the Young Adults Together

London office to officially launch Stay Strong, their exercise-for-health programme, and his devastation as he fully grasped the pain some of their clients were battling on a daily basis. The feelings of otherness, of not fitting in or belonging to the world, the loneliness. And she cried even more to read of his determination to try to reach as many people as possible, to let people know that they were loved and valued and cherished for their uniqueness.

The seventh letter was short. She read it time and time again, trying to take every word in.

Dear Alice,
Our last time together was not how things should have ended. There are so many things I still need to say to you. Will you consider meeting me in Paris? In the hope that you will, I've enclosed flight and hotel details for you.

I dearly hope you will come, but if you don't I will not write again.

I hope you find the happiness you deserve.

Thank you for a Christmas I will always cherish.
Luis

She stared at the dates on the tickets. He wanted to meet her next week, on February the fourteenth. Valentine's Day.

She held all seven letters in her hands, weighing them, weighing their significance. He had taken the time to write to her. He had made no demands. Instead his letters had been considered glimpses into his life. They had been generous and kind.

And what had she done in return? Shame crept along her limbs. She had accused him of looking for a distraction. When the same could be levelled at her. Weren't his appearance and the days they had spent together a distraction from her PhD? She had embraced his company and the chemistry between them as eagerly as he had. She had initiated and participated in all those emotionally and physically intimate moments as equally as he had. And when he had opened his heart to her, she had shut down like a coward. She hadn't trusted him enough to tell him of the fears that held her hostage to a life so carefully led it was devoid of all colour and hope.

She looked again at the flight ticket. Would she go? She stood and paced the room, a burning anger towards her dad and her own inability to leave the past behind growing in intensity.

* * *

'Are you enjoying yourself?'

Luis turned to Kara's quietly spoken question, excusing himself from the group of sports agents and travel-company CEOs he had been speaking to.

Kara waited for his answer expectantly, this party having been her idea. At the beginning, the garden party had had a dual purpose—to celebrate his World Championship win and to formally announce his appointment both as Chair of the Monrosian Sports and Tourism Department and Global Sports Ambassador for Young Adults Together. But then, realising that the party could serve a wider purpose, he had expanded its scope to act as a showcase for everything that Monrosa could offer as a sports and wellness destination.

But the party was also Kara and Edwin's way to privately acknowledge his return to Monrosa…and the family. And Kara's attempt to cheer him up. Even though he continually insisted that he was perfectly happy, they both knew that that was a lie.

He hugged Kara into him and said, 'Immensely.' He gestured about him; the palace's gardens had been transformed into a celebration of everything that was wonderful about the island. 'How couldn't I when you have given me the best party since time began?'

He might have suggested that the party celebrate Monrosa, but it had been Kara who pulled it together in his absence, as he had been travelling abroad for much of the past month, promoting the island as the perfect destination both for professional athletes and amateurs, thanks to its climate and already excellent sports facilities that would be expanded in the next five years in line with the new sustainable-tourism strategy he was devising with his senior department strategists.

In the food area, all the island's leading chefs had come together to produce a five-course tasting menu, using ingredients only sourced on the island. The food producers and their families were helping serve the food to the guests, using the opportunity to promote and educate on their produce. Local choirs and musicians were providing the entertainment. Staff and volunteers from the Monrosian Environmental Protection Agency were giving walking tours of the palace's waterfront, explaining the importance of Monrosa's unique biodiversity and Edwin's strategy for protecting it. And down by the marina, in the late evening sunshine, the various sports bodies were giving demonstrations of the facilities available in Monrosa.

Kara smiled at him, but he could tell that she didn't quite believe his insistence that he was having a good time. 'I sent Alice an invite… she messaged to say that she was tied up with her thesis.'

He shifted away from Kara, closing his eyes for a moment, letting the winter sun heat his face. Trying to shift the knot of disappointment out of his throat. He could have told Kara that Alice wouldn't respond. He had sent her numerous letters over the past month and had heard nothing in return. Not even a message telling him to stop writing to her.

It was close to six weeks since he had last seen her. On the morning of New Year's Day he had escorted her to the car that was waiting to bring her from the palace to the airport, both of them pretending that the night before hadn't happened, and that they were simply friends…or perhaps acquaintances, saying goodbye to one another after spending a few uneventful days in one another's company. They had shaken hands, kissed each other on the cheek and said goodbye, only sharing a fleeting glance before the car had pulled away.

And he had gone back into the palace and,

instead of attending his scheduled meeting with his father and Edwin to discuss his future, he had packed a bag, commandeered the royal jet and flown to Courchevel, where he had spent a week with friends. During the day he had skied every black run in the resort and by night he had partied hard. But it hadn't worked. He hadn't been able to outrun his hurt, the humiliation of having declared his one-sided love. And then there had been the guilt—the guilt of knowing that he was letting Edwin and his father down. But also the guilt that he was letting himself down. After a week he had returned to Monrosa, knowing he needed to find a new path for himself in life. One that would give him a purpose and meaning. One that might fill the vacuum inside of him.

Now he gently asked Kara, 'How are you doing?'

Kara blinked hard. 'Okay.'

He placed a hand on her shoulder and drew her into his side. Affection and concern clogged his throat.

'It's easier now that you are here,' Kara added.

A few days after he had returned to Monrosa, whilst he had still been thrashing out exactly what his role would be, his father still advocating hard for him to take a position in the treasury despite his objections, he had walked into Edwin's office and an argument between Edwin and Kara. Taken aback by how distressed they had both seemed, his first instinct had been to back out of the room, but something had told him to stay. At first they had both tried to deny that they were having an argument in the first place, and then they each claimed that the other person was overly committed to their work...and eventually, asking Kara for her permission to do so, Edwin had told him of their struggle to conceive a baby.

It had been a huge turning point in his life. Edwin and Kara confiding something so personal, trusting him with it, had deeply affected him. He saw the power and connection of family. The power of being there for one another. And, coming from that conversation, he knew he wanted to take over some of their responsibilities—in his role as Head of Sports and Tourism he would use his past experience and contacts to forge a different type of tourism, away from the mass tourism of the past to a sustainable model.

Studying him for a moment, Kara asked gently, 'And how about you, Luis—are you okay?'

A few months ago he would have made a

quip, shrugged off her question with defensive humour. But Edwin's and Kara's honesty, his own rawness since falling in love with Alice, the honesty, the truthfulness he had shared with her in the days they spent together, had him answer, 'Everything went wrong with Alice... I don't know what to do.'

'Listen to your own instinct,' Kara said, then, blinking hard, almost but not quite pushing away a gleam of tears, she added, 'There's always hope.'

He swallowed hard as he watched Kara walk away, knowing that she was thinking of her and Edwin's much longed-for baby. And then he thought about his final letter to Alice that he had sent yesterday. It was his last throw of the dice. At times he wondered why he was putting himself through all of this—what if his instinct that he had told Alice way too soon that he loved her was wrong and in fact she simply didn't love him?

He looked around the party. To the friends and colleagues and old rivals who had travelled from all over the world to celebrate with him. To the locals who had known him as a teenage rebel and had finally forgiven him for the all-night parties he had used to throw in the boat house, the noise travelling across the harbour and keeping half the city awake, causing a flurry of complaints to the palace. He saw his father and Edwin, involved in some grave discussion, his father still reluctantly letting go of power. Relationships were messy and complex...but the essence of life when you got them right.

CHAPTER ELEVEN

THE EXIT DOORS at the airport arrivals hall glided open and Alice stepped out onto the concourse on a wave of uncertainty. Should she turn around? Take the return flight back to Dublin? She studied the overhead signs, one directing her to the taxi rank, another towards Departures and the safe life she knew back in Dublin.

'Miss O'Connor, welcome to Paris. I'm here to take you to your hotel.'

She whipped around at the softly spoken words to find a tall, dark-haired man, entirely dressed in black.

'His Highness Prince Luis sent me.' He took hold of her suitcase and gestured for her to follow him.

For a moment she considered wrangling the suitcase from him, but the man was built like a tank. She was so confused, her ability to think straight a thing of the past, fear taking over instead. She wasn't even certain why she was here. She still had no faith in her judgement. But she knew she had to have some form of closure with Luis. She so desperately wanted to believe that he loved her but a voice in her head was mocking her gullibility. This wasn't how love was portrayed in the movies. This was messy and emotional and so damn scary that she was barely holding everything together.

Their car was parked directly outside the arrivals hall in a no-parking zone. Two airport security men were standing by it. For a moment she thought they were about to ticket them but instead they shook her escort's hand and wandered off. And then she realised it was a diplomatic car.

Inside the car, the driver had the engine idling. Her escort opened the rear door for her and once she was settled he sat in the front beside the driver. She studied the back of both men's heads, it slowly dawning on her that she had seen both of them in Monrosa. Of course— they were Luis's protection team.

She sank into her seat, hoping that neither of them had witnessed her ambush and kiss him that first time at Kara's wedding, or worse still had watched her drag him into the woods on New Year's Eve. They drove in silence into the centre of Paris. At her hotel, The Montclar, she was met by the general manager, who took her directly to her suite, where he informed her that His Highness Prince Luis had arranged for them to dine in an hour's time in the privacy of his penthouse suite.

She nodded and smiled, taking the access key to the private lift that serviced the penthouse, assuring him that she would make her own way there, her smile only fading as her door clunked shut.

She counted to ten. Threw off her jacket. And opened the door again and rushed to the stairwell. She bolted down the five floors and into the reception area. Two protection officers were standing at the penthouse lift. They eyed her dubiously. No doubt his dates in the past would have worn something more glamorous than just jeans and a sweatshirt. She waved the access key at them and stated her name. They exchanged a look, but then one of the men pressed the call button. The private lift arrived within seconds. And its ascent to the twentieth floor passed in the blink of an eye. She pulled back her shoulders as the doors opened, expecting to encounter yet more security personnel standing in a corridor, but instead the doors opened onto a vast sitting room. And to Luis, who was sitting at a desk, working through a pile of paperwork.

He was wearing a white open-necked shirt, the grey suit jacket lying on the arm of a sofa matching his grey trousers. Her heart fluttered and danced to see him. She closed her eyes for a moment, exasperated with herself. Her heart knew nothing. It was a soft, squidgy thing that gave way too easily to lust and easy compliments and promises.

She stepped into the room. 'I'm not in the mood for dinner.'

He stared at her.

She moved towards the desk. Folded her arms. 'So what did you want to talk about?'

'You're angry.'

'No, I'm not.'

She waited for him to say something but he just continued watching her. She clapped her mouth shut against the words bubbling inside of her desperate for an escape. She hated this new side to her, this irrational passion. Life had been so much easier before when silence had come so easily to her. But Luis had unleashed something inside of her and it scared her just how out of control it made her feel.

Why wasn't he saying anything? This meeting was his idea. He was the chatty one. The one who always knew what to say. Panicking, she turned away, afraid of the emotions she was feeling. But at the lift she spun around and admitted, 'Do you know what? Yes, I'm angry. And I hate it.' She moved across the room, stopped in front of the desk, all sense of pride abandoning her. 'I'm angry because I'm here and I don't really know why I came.'

Luis's heart was pounding. For the past week he had been dreading the prospect of Alice not turning up. He had tried preparing himself for the disappointment. And in the hope she would come he had also run through endless scenarios for how he would handle her silence and upset and wariness. But what he had not anticipated was this anger. She was practically sizzling with it. And he was at a loss as to how to deal with it.

Standing in front of him, wearing her trademark black jeans and a black sweatshirt, her silver eyes shining bright with emotion, her cheeks hot, she was throwing down a gauntlet that he didn't understand. How was he supposed to react? What was she looking for from him? He scrambled for a foothold in understanding how to react. And then the words came to him. They were on the tip of his tongue, ready to be uttered, but he held back, knowing he was possibly going to make the worst mistake of his life. He opened his mouth, his heart, his pride, and said quietly, 'You're here because you love me.'

She snorted. 'Do you reckon?' She knew she was being nasty and irrational, something deep inside of her screaming for protection.

'Being in love is scary.'

'Scary? I'll tell you what is scary.' Inside, she shouted at herself to stop. Why was she doing this? Why was she fighting him? 'Scary is not knowing if you are being duped, if you are reading a situation all wrong. Scary is never being able to trust your own judgement. Scary is being pushed to say things you're not ready to say.' She paused for a breath, the fire inside of her dimming.

'And do you know what's scary for me?' he asked. 'Not being believed in. I've spent the past twenty years fighting my father's distrust. With you, I had thought it was different.'

She swallowed at the softness of his tone, the hurt in his voice. Her heart felt swollen with fear and love and confusion. 'How can I believe you?'

He looked down at his hands clasped before

him on the desk. For a moment she had a vision of him walking towards the lift and opening its doors, telling her that their meeting was over. Panic turned her stomach over.

He lifted his head, his expression intense. 'Why can you believe me? How about the fact that you're the first person I have ever declared my love to? And not because I was scared of love in the past...but because I have never fallen for someone like I have for you.'

'We both know that your life is uncertain right now—what if you're confusing the need for certainty and security with love?'

His gaze narrowed, his expression confounded. 'I'll admit to struggling as to what my future direction would be when we met.' He flipped closed his laptop, his expression hard. 'But do you seriously think that I'm so lacking in character and self-understanding that I would open my heart to you just to have a distraction, a new purpose in life? Really? Do you think so little of me?'

His voice carried a barely contained fury. She braced herself for the fear, for the panic that always hit her when faced with another person's anger. 'Why me, Luis? There are so many other women you could have chosen.'

His mouth tightened. 'Why you? Because

you're the bravest, funniest, most intelligent, most contrary woman I have ever met.'

She stood. 'I'm a physical mess around you and I *hate* being so out of control. We could have…maybe we should have…maybe it would have doused the fire between us.'

He stood and moved around the desk with the slow, easy grace of a panther. His eyes bored into hers. 'You can say it, Alice. We should have slept together. Do you think that would have doused what's between us? It would have only made it worse. Do you think it was easy for me not to have slept with you? Do you think I didn't want to strip you naked and make love to you time and time again? Do you know how many times I fantasised about knocking on your bedroom door, or arriving on your doorstep in Dublin, and having sex with you?'

'What stopped you? Why did you push me away? Do you know how that made me feel?'

'I was trying to protect you.'

Her heart felt too big for her chest. She stepped back. Placed her hands on her hips. Testing him. Hating herself for being so needy. 'I didn't want your protection. I wanted your rawness, your desire. I yearned for you to want me without reason…the way I wanted you.'

He dipped his head, and then with a grunt he was moving towards her. He whipped her up in his arms and pushed her against the terrace door behind him, the uninterrupted view of the Eiffel Tower in the distance of no interest to either of them.

His mouth locked onto hers. His breath was hot, his tongue fierce. He wrapped her legs around his waist. She dug her fingers into his hair. Wanting to hurt him. Wanting this so badly.

He pushed up her sweatshirt, muttering a low curse on seeing her black lace bra beneath.

His mouth met hers again, his hand cupping her breast.

It was a duel of a kiss, sending her head and body spinning into a web of lust. Feeling every edge of resistance melt away, and terrified of that fact, she knew she had to test him even further. Breaking away she said, 'Admit it, this is just about lust to you. It was just a cat-and-mouse game to you, to really hook me and get me under your control.'

His hand cupped her breast even harder, and she bit his neck.

He growled. 'No! And you know that… I've never tried to control you. It's your past that's controlling you. Stop pushing me away. Believe in me. Believe in us.' He twisted his head and whispered, 'I love you…'

For a moment she considered giving in to him, giving in to what was in her heart, but the sceptic, the fighter in her, made her whisper, 'How long before you start regretting saying it, though…how long before the novelty of thinking you're in love with me wears off?' She bit down softly on his earlobe. If she pushed him away, if she forced him to see the truth of their relationship, she could save herself from the heartache of being rejected. Her dad never loved her despite all of his declarations and promises. What if Luis was the same?

He groaned. She bit down a little harder.

His thumb flicked across her nipple. Her head fell backwards as a ripple of pleasure ran through her body. 'I'm a one-woman type of guy; I'm never going to stop loving you.'

She kissed him, her mouth demanding, needing the connection her heart was too afraid to allow. What they had, the emotional connection, couldn't be real. It was too fantastical. Real life wasn't like this. Ending the kiss, she whispered, 'It's lust. Nothing more.'

His eyes met hers, passion and honour shining brightly. 'You're wrong.'

How could he be so certain? 'Aren't you scared?'

She cringed at her badly thought-out question, at the tremble in her voice. Hating the vulnerability she had failed to mask.

His forehead came to rest against hers, his unblinking autumnal eyes searching hers. 'I've never been more scared in my entire life. But for the last six weeks I have been miserable and I cannot contemplate life without you. I've missed you. I've missed your laughter, your smile, your body, the way you roll your eyes...' he paused and kissed her on the mouth, with a rough desperation she understood only too well, but when he pulled back the fire in his eyes was fading '... I've missed the sense of peace you bring to me. The calmness. The acceptance. I've been running away from myself for as long as I can remember, but with you, I've stopped running.' He paused, his voice breaking with emotion. 'Without you I'm not the person I want to be. I'm not the person I'm capable of being.'

He eased her away from the window, stepped back, but she followed and gathered him into her, her heart aching. Against his chest she whispered, 'I didn't want to believe that you loved me, because I couldn't understand why you would.' She drew back and shook her head. 'I'm an introverted control-freak virgin…could two people be more different? I'm broken, Luis. I'm not good for you. You deserve better. You deserve a woman who can love you blindly, who never doubts you.'

His hand touched her cheek. 'You are the calm to my chaos. You get me. I have never met someone who wants to know me like you do, who wants to get beneath the person I choose to show to the world.' Tension lines pulled at the corners of his eyes. 'I love you, Alice…but I need to know that you believe me when I say that. I cannot be in a relationship where I'm not believed.' He paused and planted a slow, tender kiss on her lips, his hands cupping her cheeks. 'Or in a relationship where my feelings are not reciprocated.' His voice dipped into a bare whisper. 'I understand why you are scared of love. Your dad left you so scarred by his actions I understand why you would find it difficult to love…' he stopped and let out a heavy breath, shrugging '…or perhaps I'm overcomplicating this and your feelings for me just aren't the same. Maybe I'm not enough…'

Luis waited for her to speak, his heart breaking apart. He had done it again. He had rushed in with both feet, desperate to have her know how much he loved her…but even more desperate to hear that she loved him back. He closed his eyes, cursing himself. He had sworn to himself that this meeting would be calm and unrushed. But instead it was all passion and desperation. Was he, in truth, subconsciously handing her an excuse to back out of what was between them? He turned and looked out of the window. It was starting to rain, fat raindrops running down the glass and blurring the Eiffel Tower. He walked over to the fireplace, suddenly feeling cold to the bone. He waited for her to speak, the fire behind the glass screen of the modern inset stove doing little to touch the chill in his body.

'You are enough…you are so much it scares me.' She spoke in a bare whisper, her wide eyes reflecting the fear in her voice. She came and stood in front of him, her arms wrapping about her waist. 'My dad hurt my mum so terribly, I'm terrified of ever being hurt like that.'

'I'd never—'

She interrupted him. 'I know you wouldn't. I know in my heart you wouldn't, but I have spent so many years protecting myself, hardening myself to a life where I would be alone, what happened between us was too intense for me to process.' She bit her lip, tears glisten-ing in her eyes. He went to hold her but, shaking her head, she took a step backwards. 'No. I need to explain all of this to you.' She gave a shaky laugh. 'I had my life planned out. A life with little risk of having my heart broken. And then I meet you. And I was so incredibly cross at how attracted I was to you. I watched you in Monrosa's cathedral as you stood at Edwin's side the day he married, and you whispered something to him that had him smile and relax for a few moments and I was hooked. Even from that distance I was hooked by your kindness, your empathy, your energy. And later on you tried to help me when my sandal got stuck, but I was so overwhelmed I snapped at you.' She buried her face in her hands and groaned. 'And then I ambushed you and kissed you. You must have thought that I was crazy.'

He shook his head. 'It was the most wonderful kiss of my life.'

She smiled at that. 'I love you, Luis. I love your spontaneity, your optimism. I know I might grumble about it sometimes but that's only because you are pushing me to go outside my comfort zone, something I need to do.'

He wanted to grin. He wanted to whoop. But he needed, wanted to hear more from her. 'What future do you want for us, Alice?'

She frowned. Shrugged.

He waited.

She cleared her throat. 'I'm not sure…what do you think?'

He shook his head. 'You tell me.'

She frowned even more. 'Why?'

'You said that your dad played mind games with you, manipulated things to control you. Well, I want you to be in control of how this relationship evolves.'

'But that doesn't seem right…it should be equal…it…'

He shrugged. 'I will go at your pace.'

She let out a long, deep breath. 'I love you.'

He grinned. 'So you said. Now, what about our future?'

She bit her lip again. Blushed. She tilted her chin. 'I want to make love with you. I want to move to Monrosa and be with you. I want us to marry and grow old together. I want your babies.' She stopped and looked appalled. In a rush she said, 'Oh, that's not the type of future you meant…you look so shocked!'

He shook his head, fighting for words. And then he realised that the time for speaking was over. Lifting her up into the air, he twirled her around and then, lowering her, he whispered,

'I have never heard anything so perfect in all of my life.'

He kissed her long and slow, only breaking to lift her sweatshirt off. She undid the buttons of his shirt and dropped it to the floor, her hands moving over his bare skin with a slow reverence that kicked his desire up a dangerous notch.

He undid her bra, and stood back, wanting to etch this moment on his brain for ever. When he kissed the perfect pert shape of her breast she gasped, and gasped again when he undid the button of her jeans.

She kicked off her boots as he pulled her jeans down, his hands lingering over the soft curves of her hips and bottom. He laid her down on the rug before the fire, his mouth and fingers caressing every inch of her body, her gasps, the arching of her body, the feel of her hands raking through his hair, over his shoulders, driving him on.

But then, her eyes dazed, she pushed him onto his back and fumbled for the button of his trousers, her mouth planting a hot kiss on his before she mumbled, 'I can't handle this for much longer.'

He immediately flipped her back over, caressed her cheek, his heart ready to explode as he stared into the eyes of the woman who had seen his true self, who had seen his potential, who made him a better man, and in a low growl he said, 'You can decide on what future we have, but I'm in control of this.'

Alice arched her back, warmth and need and desire leaving her barely able to think. Luis ran kisses along her collarbone, his fingers torturing her nipple. She arched even more as his mouth shifted to her nipple, the warmth, the abrasion of his tongue, sending waves of frustrated pleasure through her body. His hands moved over her stomach until he reached her panties. His fingers curled around the fabric and as her back arched in response he pulled them off, his expression fierce. She inhaled deeply, suddenly feeling really exposed. No man had seen her like this. His gaze moved up her naked body, and she blinked at the desire and love in his eyes. 'You are so beautiful.'

Her heart skipped. Her skin glowed and tingled. And she held her breath when he lowered his trousers, her body temperature soaring when he stood over her naked.

He lay down at her side, his hand running over her body in soft sweeps, and then his mouth met hers. His kiss was tender and kind, his fingers caressing. And then he gazed down at her, his expression concerned. 'I don't want to hurt you.'

She smiled at his worry, loving him even more, and whispered, 'I know, and you never will.'

She clung to him when he entered her, gasped at the wonder of their becoming one. Her body arched up to meet every inch of him. Not once did their gazes part. Her gasps were met by his whispers of love and adoration, and she came apart in his arms time and time again, but it was only when he eventually came with her, after what felt like hours of torture, that the most powerful, life-affirming surge of love split her body in two.

And afterwards they lay on the floor, covered by a throw from the sofa, and stared into each other's eyes, no words spoken, their smiles saying everything.

EPILOGUE

'DON'T CRY. THAT'S supposed to be my job today.'

Breaking away from waving at the crowds lining the streets of Monrosa's old town, Alice reached over to touch Toni's hand. Toni looked sensational in her gold bridesmaid's gown, selected to match her own backless ivory lace gown threaded with gold.

Toni flapped her hand before her eyes, laughing and crying all at once. 'I know I'm going to ruin my make-up. It's just that you look so amazing and I'm so happy for you and Luis is going to die when he sees you and everything about this day is so magical.'

Beside Alice, holding Alice's winter wedding bouquet of ruby-red, lilac and midnight-blue roses and peonies, her mum continued to wave and smile at the crowds while whispering under her breath, 'Girls, concentrate.'

Alice and Toni giggled.

Alice waved to the people of Monrosa, who had so warmly embraced her since she had moved to the island, her heart exploding as flashing images of the past year ran through her mind—a book sailing through the air this precise day a year ago. The Christmas week in London and Verbier when she had fallen in love. The day she had moved to Monrosa last April and Luis's excitement as he had shown her around their new home, a modern villa within the palace grounds overlooking the sea. Her work in establishing a palace museum. The book she was writing in conjunction with his father on the history of Monrosa. The hot summer's day when they had been out sailing on the Mediterranean and Luis had proposed to her. How her heart ached when Luis was away promoting Monrosa and Young Adults Together, her pride in how much he was already accomplishing. The thrill, the exultation, the wonder of their reunions. The long nights where they barely slept. Wanting to chat, to connect, to make slow and tender love.

A loud roar went up from the waiting crowd when their open carriage entered Plaza Santa Ana. Climbing down from the carriage, she walked towards the crowd and waved, their applause and calls of goodwill quickening her heart. Once she was certain that the crowd had had a good look at her gown she returned to the steps of the cathedral and to the Cardinal of Monrosa, who was waiting for them, accepting his welcome.

The Cardinal went inside, and they lined up. Toni, who was trembling just about as much as she was, led the way, and, clutching her mum's arm, Alice followed, unable to breathe, her legs shaking so fiercely she was worried they might buckle at any moment. She knew she should smile, should look at their waiting guests. But, totally overwhelmed, she could only focus on the never-ending length of the aisle before them.

And then he stepped out into view. And she sighed and smiled shyly. His magnificence in his navy-blue officer's dress uniform, the love singing from his eyes and his gentle smile filled her heart with joy and happiness.

Christmas miracles did happen after all.

* * * * *

*If you missed the previous story in
the Royals of Monrosa trilogy,
check out*

Best Friend to Princess Bride

*And look out for the next book
Coming soon!*

*If you enjoyed this story,
check out these other great reads from
Katrina Cudmore*

**Second Chance with the Best Man
Resisting the Italian Single Dad
Christmas with the Duke**

All available now!